You just have to take a deep breath and
then find the courage to tell yourself
that everything is going to be just fine.

This book is a work of fiction. Names, characters, places, and incidents either are the product of the author's imagination or are used fictitiously. Any resemblance to actual events or locales or persons, living or dead, is entirely coincidental.

Cover Design by Amaris I. Manning

We, pEOPLE

by Amaris I. Manning

Section 1
2012-2013

Lee,

Hey, how are you doing in Australia? I bet it's pretty nice over there and I'm sure you and your family are doing well.

Don't worry, that's not how I am going to start off every email, I promise. In fact, I don't know how I'm going to start off any of my emails because I'm still trying to get used to the idea of you not being across the street. I'm sorry, I really am, I promise. I just don't like change, and you know I don't like change. I mean, I'm okay with change, but certain things are harder to accept, you know? With school starting tomorrow, I don't know how it's going to be now that I'm going to be entering sophomore year at our high school without you by my side. It kind of sucks.

I had a strategy. Well...a thought, more so.

I believe that the idea of change scares us into wanting to do certain things that are acceptable to others, but that's how we end up doing the stupidest things. Even if we think it's okay—it's still bad because it's stupid.

I'm in way over my head, I know. I can hear you right now, telling me to get myself together and believe that things are going to be alright this year, and I want to believe you. I do. But then, something happened earlier today.

So, my mom called me downstairs and suggested for me to welcome the new neighbors to the neighborhood. That's right. A new family moved into the house where you and your family used to live before you moved to the other side of the world. Don't get me wrong, they're a nice family and they look good too, but I clearly don't like change.

Not a lot of people do. Especially when it hits you in the face like a tree branch on a car— it just comes out of nowhere.

To tell you the truth, I didn't want anything to do with the new neighbors, but it was my mother's orders. My mother's like the Mafia fused into one person. There was no compromising when it came to certain things. After all, she's still my mom. So, as the saying goes: *she brought me in this world, she'll take me out.*

So, I unwillingly went across the street to introduce myself to the new neighbors. I tried to introduce myself to them at first, but the parents kept going back and forth with each other speaking in their native language. It only took them about a minute or two to finally realize that I was standing in front of their house, waiting for their attention. They smiled. The woman introduced herself and made it clear that her name was spelled *"Robyn"* not *Robin*.

Robyn Son.

The man introduced himself as Han Son. They had a daughter named Roselle, and a son named Benton.

Roselle was very beautiful with her red dyed hair, olive skin, and brown eyes. She only gave me a head nod, like a *"wassup"*, when she saw me. Benton was something that stepped out of a miraculous painting. Well, not *miraculous*, but he sure nice-looking. Extremely nice-looking.

He has long dark hair, sharp cheekbones, dark brown eyes, and I can only imagine what his smile would've looked like if he hadn't looked so expressionless and wasn't so rude. Regardless, they were a nice-looking Asian family with some good genes. (Somewhere within the conversation, Robyn mentioned that they were Korean.)

Anyway, Robyn asked me about the high schools within the area, wondering which ones were decent enough to send their kids. Personally, I didn't know nor did I care. I mean, didn't they do their research before settling in? When my mom and I moved into our house, a couple months after my parents split, my mom had already looked up and found the best schools in the area. That's how you and I met—good ol' H.J Pickerson Middle School.

Now I have to suffer a second year of dealing with the delinquents of Gabe-Day High School. But, even though the students were infuriating, Gabe-Day was a pretty good school—academically. I told Robyn that the teachers were pretty flexible and the classes weren't so bad. Plus, Principal Vickins was the best principal on the East Coast. (Remember how last year she did a lip-sync battle against Mr. Enrique and Counselor Rashad to celebrate the end of the year? Classic.)

I also told her that Gabe-Day had a lot of extracurricular programs. She just smiled as I went on and on.

"We started a STEM program mid-last year because of a robotics program we entered," I said. "It was pretty cool, I liked it. But I was mainly involved with our theater program. We did the musical *Birds* as our spring production." *And boy it was a shit-show.* We didn't even get in half the amount of people we had attend the fall production.

Robyn started telling me about how she wanted Benton to be more involved in extracurricular activities, and how she wanted him to become more acquainted with people within his age group. The usual concerns of a mother for her child.

I gave Robyn Counselor Rashad's contact information in order for her to discuss her son's possible enrollment.

"I would send Counselor Rashad an email as soon as you can and then a text", I sighed, "and then a phone call a few hours after the text message. Followed by another email."

Out of nowhere, Robyn hugs me. I get that I was helpful, but we had just met. I couldn't just push her off me though. Last thing I wanted to do was make a terrible impression of myself.

When I came back into the house after talking with Robyn, my mom was sitting on the couch. She asked how it went with the new neighbors, and I told her everything was fine. That's what I wanted to believe, but I just don't know about school tomorrow. It's all one big oof.

Your friend,

Meagan Wright

Lee,

This morning, Principal Vickins made everyone take a health exam before the start of classes, which was dumb and completely unnecessary.

I'm not just saying that because I hate getting my weight checked. I'm just speaking for everyone when I say that it was a complete waste of time. The first day of school is always the hardest because teachers have to go over the syllabus, and then you have to make sure you have the right supplies in order to pass the class. It's enough to make anyone's blood pressure spike.

Thankfully, when it was my turn to get examined by the nurse, I was in and out. I already accepted my weight, which wasn't as bad as I thought. I've eventually become comfortable with my size once I made the goal to be healthy, not skinny. I'm always going to be a curvy girl, and I'm okay with being a size 12/14. I'm just trying to be more active in order to live longer, that's all. Plus, staying active and watching how much I eat will help me with my heart condition. So there's that as well. (In case you forgot, I was born with Prolonged QT Syndrome. It's genetic—came from my mom's side of the family.)

Anyway, after I was done my health examination, I was able to head to Counselor Rashad's office to receive my roster for this year. Students were coming in and out of his office like chickens. When I walked in, he was on the phone, talking to a parent most likely. He was rolling his eyes, shaking his head. He gestured for me to come in and handed me my roster.

He lowered the phone from his face. "You have until the end of the week to drop and add classes and adjust your roster." His accent gets thick whenever he's annoyed. Whoever he was talking with on the phone was really getting on his last nerve.

I had the chance to look at my schedule before the first bell rang. I have to say, my classes are way better this year, which I was not expecting:

ROSTER 2012-2013:

1. **HNR ALGEBRA II: 9:04 – 10:04, MORENO, ENRIQUE**
2. **ENGLISH II: 10:10 – 11:10, ACOSTA, ROVER**
3. **ART 101: 11:15 – 12:15, BISONNETTE, JEAN**
4. **LUNCH: 12:20 – 1:30**
5. **CHEMISTRY: 1:40 – 2:40, REYNOLDS, KATHY**
6. **PERSONAL FINANCE: 2:50 – 3:45, VALENTINA, RAY**

Mr. Rover is probably one of the best teachers I've ever had. I had him last year for my English 101 course and he was amazing.

Mr. Enrique is pretty cool too, but he likes to mess with his students a lot, calling them out on little things. The one thing that really bugs me about Mr. Enrique more than anything is that he gives us assigned seats. So it was no surprise that as soon as I walked into his classroom, he already had a seating chart displayed on the projector-screen.

I realized that I was seated right behind Allie Montgomery from the theater club last year. I immediately thought of asking Mr.

Enrique if I could switch seats with someone else, but I figured that he'd refuse.

I had no other option but to just shut up and deal with it for the rest of the school year. It wasn't that I despised Allie, she was a nice girl, but she was so annoying. And dippy. Seriously. Her voice reminded me of chalk scratching against a chalkboard, and whenever she tried to speak louder to recite her lines, I would close my eyes and pray to God that I wouldn't end up going deaf.

Even our theater director, Dexter, started to consider her for more silent roles that were also relevant since Allie is known for being a diva when it comes to casting.

Anyhow, class hadn't started yet, so I decided to turn my attention to this book I started reading by Jace Gregg, one of the best novelist of our time. Two of his books that you've probably heard of have been adapted into movies this past year:

The Heartbeat Upbeat and *The Infinite Dynamic of Claud & Francis*.

(Very good books by the way, highly recommend.)

I started reading his book *Chasing Aubrey Hunter* sometime last week, and I was already on the tenth chapter. I had about thirty more chapters to go. It's a really good book, although the first couple of chapters were so friggin' slow that I thought I was going to lose my mind. Although, unlike the other books I've read by Jace Gregg so far, *Chasing Aubrey Hunter* is mainly full of suspense than romance, which I love.

While I was reading my book, Allie Montgomery took it upon herself to turn around and face me with those big owl-like eyes of hers. I shifted my attention to her, still keeping my book over my face.

Dramatically, Allie greeted me and was like, "Hiiii there! I'm Allie Montgomery. You must be a new girl, yeah? Where you from?"

I had two options: I could've just ignored her and read my book, or, I could've just played along because she's obviously too dim-witted to realize that she's not funny. Still, that wouldn't have been fair to me because then I'd be the one losing precious *Hank-time*. (Hank's the protagonist in *Chasing Aubrey Hunter*.)

Yet, I spoke to Allie anyway.

"Allie. It's me. Meagan Wright." Pause. "We did the fall play and spring musical together last year for theater. I was News-Anchor Mindy for the play *Weatherman*, and I played Gozo the Parrot in *Birds*." A blank stare was all I got from her.

I could've just given up and went back to reading, but I wasn't going to suddenly become the "new girl" because of pea-brained Allie spreading rumors that I was new when in fact I wasn't. So, I pulled out the big guns.

"I'm '*Agron Melhart: Black Edition*'."

She then gasped and finally a light-bulb went off. She was like, "Ooooh! Riiiight! Now, I remember you!"

In case you forgot, for Halloween last year, I decided to be Agron Melhart from the supernatural, sci-fi series *Allegiance Society*, the greatest manga-turned-anime series to ever exist.

(Agron Melhart is one of my favorite characters from the series, and I'm not just saying that because he's one of the main characters and is aligned with the Werewolf Circle. Aside from Agron, I also love Renei. She's one of the only two hybrids within the series and she's friggin' epic. Every time she appears in a scene, she's dynamite, but the show kind of does her dirty because unlike the manga, her character growth isn't shown as much compared to the manga. On the show, they just make her seem like the flip-flopping bad guy that only does good unless it benefits her alone.)

But me being Agron Melhart for Halloween last year—it totally backfired. At first I was fine. I was looking good, wearing his signature ivory battle cloak and cream combat bodysuit that I ordered half-price from Costume-Extravaganza-dot-Com.

It's legit. I even wore his signature glasses too. Even though Agron's a dork, he's a cool dork who knows how to fight and use his shifting abilities.

But while I was thinking that things were great and that I was looking good, people thought I was weird and couldn't piece together who I was supposed to be. That was until I told them. But only if they asked.

Oddly enough by the end of the day, I became known as '*Agron Melhart: Black Edition*'. So yeah.

Anyway, class had eventually started after God knows how long and Allie had lost interest in talking to me, which was fine to me. But then, as I'm getting all settled in and ready to focus on whatever Mr. Enrique was planning to teach the class, some boy next to me had tapped my shoulder, asking if I had a pencil that he could borrow.

Like, dude are you kidding me?

13

Still, I lent him one of my pencils.

He just took it with a smile and winked. "*Gracias, chica.*"

I nodded as he turned away.

Not going to lie, he was pretty cute. I figured that he must've been a senior because I could tell he had gradually overcame that awkward puberty stage.

The boy's hair was short and dark, kept slicked back, his eyes were honey brown, and he had a dimpled smile that made him look childlike. He's got a nice build on him too, but I didn't want to get caught staring. I turned my focus back to whatever Mr. Enrique was blabbing about.

I suddenly heard the boy softly chuckle and I could feel him looking at me from the corner of his eye. I looked. He had his elbows propped on the desk with his hands folded together over his mouth to hide the smirk on his face. His eyes were definitely on me.

It was extremely weird that he kept staring at me but I did my best not to pay him any mind. Well, that was until he leaned over towards me and whispered, "It's okay to want a picture, *chica*. I ain't gonna judge." He had some nerve.

I felt my lips part open and my eyebrows furrowed.

Was this dude for real?

I scoffed. "You're really trying aren't you?."

"Who says I am?" He winked before drifting his eyes to the book in my lap. "Jace Gregg, huh? You're not one of those girls that's an instant sucker for an unrealistic love story, are you?" He spoke with such disdain in his voice that it made it difficult for me

14

to not show how my annoyance.

"And if I was?" I really wasn't.

The dude chuckled. "I'll take that as a '*no*'." A shrug. "Fair enough. I'm not much of a reader myself, but I ain't gonna judge." He leaned back into his seat and dotted his attention back to Mr. Enrique so we wouldn't get caught for chit-chatting, even though the boy did start it.

I made sure that I was facing forward so that way if Mr. Enrique did happen to say something, I wouldn't be the one to blame. But the boy was like a mesmerizing distraction. Every time he spoke, I just had to engage with him rather than focus on the teacher.

Then, the boy asks me, "Ever read RJ Bellen or Adrian Ivanov? They make Jace Gregg seem like a children's book writer if you ask me. Unpopular opinion, I know."

Now he definitely had my attention because as you know, I find RJ Bellen's works to be absolutely riveting. For a guy who claimed that he *"wasn't much of a reader"*, he sure had an odd liking for RJ Bellen. Everyone knows that Bellen is one of the most profound authors known worldwide. Some of her books have been banned in different countries due to the content being too "explicit" and "insensitive". But in reality, she was providing readers insight on the world we live in through fictional characters.

It was like: *Rise and shine! Take some notes while you're at it!*

Anyway, the boy had finally introduced himself.

"Donald Gonzalez at your service."

You're probably thinking right now: *Shut the front door! Are you kidding right now?*

I can assure you that I am far from joking. I felt stupid for not realizing who he was right from the start.

Everyone in this school knows that name.

Donald friggin' Gonzalez.

Despite the fact that he's considered short for a guy, standing roughly around 5'5" or 5'6", his mouth makes him seem much bigger, which is probably why people talk about him the way they do. Yet, he's also one of the top students of the senior class. It was rumored that he was supposed to be salutatorian, but instead, he was just like, *"Screw it!"*. People thought he was crazy, but it didn't make him any less academically inclined.

I kept my cool when he introduced himself, and I told him, "Charmed". I was just trying to get my focus back on the lesson before Mr. Enrique scolded me for not paying attention.

But once the bell had rung, signaling the end of first period, Donald picked up the conversation and rambled like a runaway train. It wasn't much of a conversation since he was just going on about nonsense that I can hardly remember. Then he finally decides to ask me for my name.

I told him, "Meagan Wright", and he smirked.

"I bet some people call you *'Meg'* or something like that?"

"Not really, no." I wasn't trying to be sarcastic.

He was saying way too much, asking way too much.

I hardly knew this guy, and yet he was acting as though we were old friends or something.

Out of the blue, he says to me, "You seem alright to me, Meagan. How about you call me whatever you'd like as the perfect trade off."

"Trade off?" I asked.

"Sure," he said, sounding enthusiastic about it. "I just thought of a potential nickname for you, and now you can call me whatever you want." He was so weird. "In fact, let me give you some help."

He started telling me the different names people would usually call him, most of them being pure insults. Still, he has thick skin so it didn't really bother him. In fact, he was smirking like a child at some of the names, giggling like a moron. It's hard to believe that he is one of the top students of his class.

Once he finished telling me the ridiculous nicknames people would call him, I let out a sigh. But what's funny is that none of the names seemed like nicknames. They were just insults. A nickname would be something that made sense and was relevant to his name, like '*Donny*' or something.

I told him, "I'm surprised no one's ever thought of '*Donny*'."

He looked at me, wrinkling his brows. "'*Donny*'? Really?"

I shrugged. "Yeah. I mean, isn't it obvious? It kind of makes sense since it's short for your name, so."

He started nodding his head. "Huh, well then. I guess you'd be the first then." He had a cheeky grin on his face that showed off his dimples.

He was obviously attractive but he didn't have to rub it in with that friggin' smile. That smile—it'd probably win anyone over. I looked away from him because I feared that I was going to start daydreaming while staring at him. I wanted to get away from him. Give him a head nod, tell him to have a nice day, and then bounce. But he didn't make things so easy. He was relentless.

I tried heading for the door once class was over, but he shifted over to stand in front of me.

He then asked, "What lunch period you got, *chica*?"

My body sort of froze. It seemed as though this would never end with him. Like I said—*relentless*.

I just made something up, hoping it would get him off my case, but it was no use. I told him that I wasn't so sure, and he offered to check my roster. I told him it was fine but he reached for it anyway, saying it wasn't a big deal.

I said nothing.

A smirk immediately popped up on his face and his eyes sort of lit up. It's hard to imagine but it really did happen.

"I'll be damned. Fourth period just like me." He then handed me back my roster, and I felt my throat become dry. "I'll see you there then. Non-negotiable." He winked, clicking his teeth before heading out the door.

I watched him leave and I snorted.

What the actual hell? This was some bullshit.

I hadn't asked for any of this. All I wanted to do was go to class and not deal with anyone.

By the time lunch rolled around, I was aching with anxiety. In the back of my mind, I thought that there were more freshmen enrolled this year compared to last year. Almost every table was practically full. Last year, there were like one or two empty tables available. Then again, last year, we had a later lunch period and not many students had the later lunch period.

So anyway, I was sitting by myself at a lunch table. I was reading my book while listening to some music. Then, out of the blue, someone knocked on the table. I looked up and saw Donny staring at me with that cheeky grin on his face again. (I call him *Donny* now I guess. He likes it, so it's whatever.)

"Mind if I join you, *chica*?" He sounded so certain that I was going to let him. I didn't want him to, but he just sat himself right across from me without warning.

As he was sitting down, he got a text message. He let out a groan, throwing his head down on the table. I looked at him.

He looked back up at me and cleared his throat. "Sorry, it's just my sister that's all. She's being a little annoying."

His sister. His *twin* sister, in fact. Morris-Lina. I've heard of her but never actually knew her. (He told me that their parents were actually expecting a boy, but when they saw it was a girl, they added *Lina* at the end to make it sound better. It's weird.)

She also goes to our school.

But as we were sitting and while Donny was talking, I noticed a tattoo on his forearm of the crescent arrow, which was the marking of the Hunter Circle from *Allegiance Society*.

I gasped. I could hardly believe it.

"Is that the Hunter's mark?" I asked, excitement being heard within my words.

Donny looked at the tattoo and then back at me. "The same one as Jaxton Chyd? Hell yeah it is."

My eyes were wide. I couldn't believe what I was hearing. He too watches *Allegiance Society!* I never would've guessed.

"You watch *Allegiance Society* too?"

He scoffed. "Anyone who doesn't is a total wimp."

I snickered. Turns out, Donny watches *Allegiance Society* religiously and was also annoyed by the way last season ended. Major cliffhanger, absolute cruelty by the writers.

We spent most of the lunch period talking about *Allegiance Society*, and I even had him take the official Alliance Aptitude quiz on his phone. Turns out, he's a Hunter. I wasn't surprised. He does seem like a strategist and doesn't seem afraid of taking risks. Not to mention that he's also a bit cocky since he wouldn't stop boasting about being a Hunter.

Hunters can be annoying from time to time.

Unfortunately, our conversation came to an abrupt end when Nathan Hendricks came up to our table, unexpectedly.

I don't know if you remember this, but Nathan and I had one class together last year. He was a pretty decent guy unless his half-witted girlfriend, Diana Clovis, was around. He could've done so much better. He's one of the best players on the lacrosse team and managed to keep all his brain cells intact. Much like Donny, Nathan's one of the top students of their class, and he has a bunch of scholarships lined up for him from some of the best colleges and universities in the country.

If only Diana was out of the picture, he wouldn't act like such a douchebag sometimes. He's not completely awful but he easily succumbs to Diana's wicked power. He just loses his guard whenever they're together and he becomes this 6'3" blonde douchebag with the typical pretty boy looks.

Anyway, Nathan came over to us with a twisted grin on his face and he quickly looked back to his giggling friends and his girlfriend. He turned his attention back to me, completely dismissing Donny's existence, and he asked me, "Wanna hang?"

This was definitely some stupid dare. There's no way Nathan would come over here ask me something like that with his girlfriend looking on.

Before I could get a word out for myself, Donny cleared his throat to get Nathan's attention.

Donny was like, "Yo *cochino*, lay off will ya? I mean, c'mon, I wouldn't want my friend to start off her year by contracting some disease that you got from Diana. You know, considering how well your girl gets around when she ain't too satisfied with you."

In the blink of an eye, Donny was knocked out of his seat. Students started huddling over to the table as Nathan and Donny went at each other like dogs in a cage fight. I was quick to make sure that I didn't get knocked out myself. I was pushing through the crowd, trying to get away from all the action.

Fortunately, one of the cafeteria supervisors had taken immediate notice of the swarm of students huddled around the table. He sprinted over, shimmying through the crowd of students, and he was able to break up the fight.

Both boys had given their all. Their clothes were wrinkled, hair ruffled, and small drips of blood coming from their mouths and noses. Nathan was bound to have a black-eye after how hard

Donny managed to slug him in return. Meanwhile, Donny was spitting out bits of blood into the trash can.

The bell sounded, signaling for the end of our lunch period. Everyone gradually dispersed to their classes as the next group of students had entered the cafeteria.

Nathan purposely bumped into Donny as he headed out the cafeteria. Donny chuckled to himself. I grabbed Donny's bookbag for him as he gently dabbed his bloody lip with the napkin I had given him. He glanced up at me as he tossed the napkin into the trash can, asking for his bookbag. I watched as he slipped on his bookbag, wincing. He tried feigning a smile, but he was terrible at hiding his pain.

Donny then threw his arm around me as we started to walk to our classes. I asked him if he was alright and sighed.

"Don't worry too much about me, kid, alright?"

"I'm not worried, just making sure you're good."

"Hm. If you say so."

"But I am."

He chuckled. "Alright, alright, I was just teasing, kid."

I wanted to tell him so badly to stop calling me 'kid'. He wasn't that much older than me. Yet, he claimed that him calling me "kid" was similar to me calling him "Donny".

He thought it was fair.

After school, Donny offered me a ride home since the ride was on the way to his house. He owned an old-fashioned black Cadillac, similar to the one my grandfather once owned. Only difference was that Donny's wasn't a convertible. Apparently,

Donny's car has been passed down from generation to generation, and now, it was his precious treasure.

"My *abuelo* always believed that the way you treat your car reflects how you'd treat your lady. If you treasure it always like a gem, you'll live a happy life. But if you bring harm towards it, you'll be on the brink of divorce and die alone."

Judging from the way Donny kept his car, I could tell that he'd treat his woman like a goddess. Everything was well-kept and polished, both inside and out. When I complimented on how nice his car looked, Donny said that he liked his car the same way he liked women: "Beautiful and bright, both inside and out."

Very well said.

Anyway, I gotta get some sleep. G'night.

Your Friend,

Meagan Wright

Lee,

Today, I met Donny's twin sister, Morris-Lina. He and I went over to his place after school so we could study for our upcoming math quiz for Mr. Enrique's class.

Even though I was aware of who she was, Morris-Lina still introduced herself to me since I was a fresh face.

"Why I'm Morris-Lina, my darling." She feigned a terrible English accent as she took a dramatic bow. When we made eye contact, she laughed and draped her arm over my shoulders. "Your face is iconic. But seriously, call me *'Moe'*. Non-negotiable."

Donny groaned out of annoyance and attempted to drag his sister away, but she just shrugged him off her. The look Moe gave him almost killed me. It was like a mixture of confusion and her being ten seconds away from socking him into next week. I tried not to laugh and covered my mouth with my hand to hide the inevitable smile creeping on my face.

Meanwhile, Donny was getting more and more annoyed by her presence as he tried to have us left alone.

"C'mon *bruja*, beat it."

Moe's eyes widened. "*Bruja!* Who you callin' *'bruja'*?" She then called him something in Spanish that really got under his skin and made his face red. He flipped her off.

Moe just rolled her eyes and yawned dramatically, unfazed. She then cut her eyes to me and smirked, deviously. I was about ready

24

to just leave and head home to study on my own, but she inched closer to me, asking whether or not I found her presence appalling.

It was weird. My throat felt dry.

I told her, "No", and she laughed.

"A'ight, I'll let you two love birds have the space." She winked at Donny, who was already bubbling with frustration. When Moe got to the stairs, she called out, "Bro! If you're able to get some, just remember to use protection, alright?!" She darted straight up the steps when Donny sprinted halfway up the stairs after her.

Moments like that made me appreciate the fact that I was an only child. I don't think I'd be able to handle the pressures of having a sibling. I know that having a sibling can be a good thing in terms of having a life-long bond with someone other than your parents, but it can be difficult.

Maybe. I doubt I'll ever know for sure.

Donny and I decided to study in the garage, which seemed like a strange place to study, but it was actually the best place in the house. The garage didn't look like any garage I've seen before. There were little decorative lights hanging all over the walls, a wide sofa by the steps, a large black and red knitted rug underneath the round table in the center, a cooler in the corner by the garage door, and two leather reclining chairs across from the sofa. There was a record player near the sofa and shelves of CDs, vinyl records, and books on the walls.

I was so marveled that Donny told me to close my mouth, or else I might swallow a fly.

As we sat down on the couch and started to study, Donny had apologized for his sister's behavior. He was like, "She's not always like this, I promise you."

Then I told him, "She's got a personality. I think it's alright."

"You're the first then." An unexpected warm smile crossed his face and I mirrored his smile in return.

He had a nice smile that I couldn't help to smile back. Plus, it was nice of him to think I was a decent person.

Even though I'm very observant, I try not to be a judgmental bitch. It's very difficult to be able to differentiate being judgmental from being observant, sometimes.

As we were studying, I ended up meeting Donny's parents. His mom came into the garage and introduced herself, insisting for me to call her by her name, Luciana, since 'Mrs. Gonzalez' made her feel old. His father, however, didn't care if I called him by his name—Nicolás—or not.

They were very nice people, and his mom started to ask me questions about how Donny and I knew each other. Donny groaned. He told her that we were trying to study for a test. I could see the redness of his cheeks as his mother continued to ask questions anyway.

Mr. Gonzalez slowly guided his wife back into the house, leaving Donny and me alone once again. Donny's mom had called out something to him in Spanish that made Donny's whole face flush. I've never seen anyone go red so much.

I immediately asked him if he was alright since his cheeks were so red. He snorted, shaking his head.

"It's warm in here. I'm wearing a leather jacket for Heaven's sake." He took off his jacket and threw it on the other end of the couch. "Better. Let's carry on, *chica*."

He was determined to move past what just happened.

It was kind of funny.

It soon started to get dark outside and we eventually decided to call it a night. Donny offered to take me home, and as we were getting ready to leave, his mom tried to get me to stay for dinner. Donny spoke up for me, telling her that I had a strict curfew and needed to get home ASAP. While that was true, he didn't have to make it seem like I didn't want to stay. But then he told me that he was more concerned about his family scaring me off.

"Trust me, kid. I'm doing you a favor," he whispered as he threw on his leather jacket. "Maybe after our second late-night study session."

I scoffed. "Since when did you start calling the shots?"

A slight grin curled on his face as he opened the front door for me. "Since now." He winked, clicking his teeth.

As I made my way to Donny's car, Moe called out my name as she ran up to me. She was panting a bit once she came up to me, and then asked if she could see my phone for a second. She could tell I was a little skeptical and she let out a sigh.

"I swear on my *abuelo's* grave that if it seems like I'm being sketchy, you have the right to slap me silly." She kept her hand over her heart to ensure her honesty.

I looked back at Donny as he looked down, holding his head in annoyance. Still, I gave her my phone and watched as she saved her phone number on my phone. Once she was finished, she handed me my phone back and playfully punched my arm.

She then looked at Donny. "Don't kill her, dipwad. Mom says be back in twenty."

"You got it," he groaned as the two of us got into the car.

I pretended not to notice the redness of Donny's cheeks as Moe winked at him. I watched as she ran back inside the house. Donny cleared his throat, trying to get himself together as he started the engine. He then asked me if I was alright and I looked at him, nodding.

He gave me a look. "You bluffing on me?"

I shrugged. "I dunno, am I?"

"Quit being cute." And with that, he turned on the radio and pulled off to drop me off home. His family seemed nice.

Really, they were.

Your Friend,

Meagan Wright

Lee,

Mr. Rover received a call this morning during class, and he told me that I was asked to head down to the main office to Principal Vickins's office.

I felt everyone staring at me as I gathered my things and headed out the door. Everyone always gets nosy whenever someone is asked to go down to the main office—it's annoying. But as I left, I heard Mr. Rover call out for the class to hush-up and pay attention to the lecture. He was a real one, I swear.

As I headed down to the main office, I kept wondering why Principal Vickins would've wanted to speak with me. I was a good student with good grades and I always kept to myself.

So, it wasn't like I was trouble.

When I made it to the office, Mrs. London told me to take a seat and informed me that Principal Vickins would be ready for me "*in a minute*". (It was actually fifteen minutes.) Mrs. London then offered me a peppermint square and I gradually took one from the jar on her desk. Mrs. London is such a nice lady. She always keeps her desk nice and tidy with a few African knick-knacks on display.

I also like how she dresses. She always wears long dresses and keeps her hair wrapped up in a printed headwrap that matches whatever she's wearing. She'll even wear some bling to go with her outfit. She's truly the fashion icon of Gabe-Day.

Anyway, Principal Vickins finally called me into her office and I felt my pulse spike. It's always nerve-wracking going into the principal's office, and it becomes even more nerve-wracking when your principal has the taxidermy of a lion's head mounted on the wall behind her.

And then Principal Vickins had the audacity to ask me, "Isn't it lovely?", when referring to her mounted lion's head. I told her, "Sure, totally", when for a fact, I was petrified. The eyes followed you when you moved.

Anyway, Principal Vickins explained to me why she called me down to her office in the first place. So, remember that new family that moved into your house across the street from my house? Well, the son was enrolled in the school yesterday and today was his first day. Principal Vickins thought that I should be his guide for the week since she believed I *"exemplified a responsible student with dignity and poise"*. Her words, not mine.

I was thinking about telling her "no" since I didn't really know the neighbor's son all too well. Plus, I'm sure he didn't want to get to know me. He was very stand-offish when we first met. He just looked at me as if he had forgotten how to speak and wanted nothing to do with me. Some charmer.

My mom always says, *"first impressions are lasting impressions"*.

Principal Vickins called the boy into her office, and as soon as he came in we made eye-contact. I regretted it almost immediately. Principal Vickins took it upon herself to introduce us to each other. (Although we already met before.)

"Benton Son this is Meagan Wright, she will be your guide for this week until you are comfortably settled into the school. Meagan this Benton Son, he will be your shadow."

Benton and I shook hands. In the back of my mind, I was planning on making a run for it, but that would've been pointless.

After Principal Vickins gave Benton his schedule, I showed Benton around the school for a bit before it was time for third period. I managed to show him the basic areas—the bathrooms, the cafeteria, the auditorium, and since we had some extra time, two of our science labs.

"If you're lucky and get Mister Jess for bio, you'll be having classes outside more so than inside," I said. "He's very experimental when it comes to science."

Benton nodded. "That's good, yeah?"

I shrugged. "He likes exploring what's beyond the textbook. I never had him but I heard he's pretty cool."

I could tell Benton was nervous. He had every right to be, though. It was his first day.

I took a quick look at his schedule as the bell sounded off, signaling the end of second period. "For second period, you got Mister Yuen for Global Literacy. Now we're into third period, so you have Psychology 101 with Missus Castello. She's great. Her class is on the third floor, left hallway, second door from the bathroom."

He nodded, telling me, "Thanks." I nodded.

I quickly headed down to Mr. Rover's room and saw my belongings in the tote that he kept right outside of his classroom. When I grabbed my bookbag, I noticed a sticky note attached to one of the straps: *Book reflection due 12-15. Your book has already been assigned and has been given-- R. Acosta.*

I looked into the tote and saw one other item that I assumed was my assigned book. I almost flipped when I realized that it was *The Infinite Dynamic of Claud & Francis* by Jace Gregg. Even though I've read it once before, it's been a while. Only Mr. Rover would assign me a book that would catch my interest.

I raced up to the fifth floor to get to my art class. Not only is Mr. Bissonnette an impatient man, but he'll never hesitate to call out a student for being late. I didn't want to be one of those students, so, I was booking it. I found an empty seat towards the back and I shared a table with Preston Highmore.

Preston and I did theater together last year, and our acquaintanceship is basically built on mutual understanding. We weren't best friends but we respected each other's personal space, and we never share our personal business with each other. He usually talks to Jordan Q. about all his personal business. (She also does theater, FYI.)

But even though we were cool with each other, there's only so much sarcasm I can take from him. But the only reason why he's so sarcastic almost all the time is because of all the crap he's been putting up with since he came out last year.

He didn't say it out in the open under his free-will, though. One day after school, a couple of guys from the lacrosse team were heading to the field for practice and they saw Preston making out with some guy while hiding under the bleachers. Then, all hell broke loose. But Preston just rolled with it. He didn't care what people thought about him. He was still the same mono-toned Preston Highmore, who wears oversized hoodies and hardly gives a crap about anything. What a guy, right?

As I sat next to Preston, he pressed his lips together in a weak smile. I could tell he was very tired. He was never much of a morning person. I wasn't either. People who can tolerate being up for long hours during the day are pretty much superhuman. Although, no matter the time of the day, Preston was always up for a debate.

He would debate with anyone about anything if the subject caught his interest. He would often get into debates with teachers, especially with Mr. Bissonnette. He and Mr. Bissonnette never saw things eye-to-eye. Like last year, Preston and Mr. Bissonnette debated on the costume designs for *Birds* and Dexter finally decided to let Jordan S. and Jordan Q. design the costumes. Mr. Bissonnette was in charge of set designing, and Preston was responsible for memorizing his lines.

It was pretty interesting watching and listening to Preston debate on something. He was so passionate and always believed he was right. Even if he was wrong about something, he still stood by whatever he had said, and he'd never admit when he was wrong.

It made him a clever jerk.

During class, Preston and I didn't talk much.

Mr. Bissonnette tasked everyone in our class to draw anything that came to our minds, as long as it wasn't inappropriate. However, we had to draw using ink and a stencil. I drew a picture of a landscape and it looked like crap at first, but, it eventually came together the more I concentrated. Meanwhile, Preston's artwork looked stellar compared to mine. He usually does his best artwork when he's *attempting* to have a good day.

Preston and I eventually started talking to each other, and he told me that Jordan Q. had set him up on a blind date with one of her co-workers from Red Pepper's Restaurant and Bar. Preston should have been thrilled, but he wasn't. He wasn't much of a *"surprise-me"* type of guy, and he wasn't down for dating random guys he didn't know.

"Jordan Q. thinks this guy will be good for me, even though I told her that there wasn't a chance in hell for us," he said, shrugging his shoulders.

I sighed as I continued my drawing. "Are you not ready to date?" It was probably a stupid question.

Preston focused on his sketch as he answered, "I don't like having conversation unless it's necessary. Do I *really* seem like dating material?" Basically his way of saying: *That's a dumb question.*

The bell eventually sounded and I gathered my things, heading out of the room without a second thought. Normally I don't question people, so why would I question Preston? I felt like a dunderhead. You never question Preston Highmore, he'll make you feel like an idiot. Unless you're Jordan Q., of course.

The rest of my day flew by smoothly and I was all set on going home. Still, I had to wait for Benton since I was still his guide, and so, I needed to hear his feedback about his classes and whatnot.

So, I waited. And I waited. And I waited until he finally showed up. Benton looked tired and was practically dragging his feet as he approached me.

"Rough day?"

He shrugged his shoulders and began to pull his hair back into a ponytail so it was out of his face. "It was good, just long." He pushed open the door, allowing me to go through first. "You?"

"Can't complain." *Far better than yours by the looks of it.*

I asked him who he had for his final class period and he showed me his schedule. My eyes widened and I covered my mouth to prevent myself from laughing. It was no wonder he looked so out of it. For sixth period, he had Mr. Aziz for Health and Fitness, and his final class period was Calculus with Mr. Webb. Those two are merciless.

No wonder Benton looked practically dead. Mr. Aziz probably put him through hell, making him do drills. Then, he had to also deal with Mr. Webb shoving a bunch of equations into his head in one sitting. Poor kid.

I had both teachers last year, so I understood his pain.

Mr. Webb had a tendency to call you out for no reason. The man would also ask you ridiculous questions that had nothing to do with the lesson, and if you couldn't answer them, he would write you up for not paying attention, even if you were.

But Mr. Aziz was the worst.

All the students call him *'Hell's Spawn'*, but it's more so out of fear than spite. Mr. Aziz could care less if you broke your arm or twisted your ankle, he would still put you to work. And if you refused, he would write you up and send you to the main office. Not only that, he'd put you through literal hell and make you do double the drill sets, even if you were on the brink of tears.

How is a guy like that even married?

Aside from all that, Benton claimed that he had a pretty okay first day of school. We were on our way to the train station when his sister, Roselle, pulled up to us in her car, and then she spoke to him in Korean. He looked at me, not knowing what to say at first, but then he cleared his throat.

He said that he would see me at school tomorrow before getting into the car, reluctantly. I felt Roselle's eyes pierce into my soul the longer she glared at me.

I watched as she drove off with Benton in the car.

Had I done something wrong?

I can still feel her eyes on me, even now while I'm home.

Your Friend,

Meagan Wright

Lee,

Principal Vickins called everyone into the auditorium for an announcement regarding an incident that involved a couple of students from our school, and a group of students from Lincoln Freedman High School, which is in South Philly.

Here's what happened: someone from Lincoln Freedman posted a comment on social media about someone from our school. Then, someone from our school responded to the same comment, calling out the student from Freedman. Then, yesterday, a few students from Lincoln Freedman jumped a few students from our school at the train station and a huge fight broke out. The fight was so bad that the police had to get involved. Someone even threatened that they had a gun but it was never clarified who made the threat or if it was true.

My thing is, why are you coming all the way from South Philly to North Philly just to pick a fight? It's not that deep.

Principal Vickins said that she's discussing things with the principal of Lincoln Freedman and expects all of us to head straight home after school. She also recommended for us to come to school with a casual shirt in order for us to change out of our uniform shirts before leaving the premises as a precaution.

"I'm not encouraging fear here," she said. "It's just an idea. If you feel that you have nothing to worry about, then okay. But if you want to be real careful, then you have the option of wearing a shirt of any kind before coming and leaving school."

Everyone knew Principal Vickins cared about us—she was like everyone's mom, pretty much. And if we had to change our shirts to prevent getting blindsided by a bunch of cowards that were too afraid to fight a fair fight, then so be it.

Principal Vickins ended the assembly by fourth period, and as Benton and I were heading to lunch, Donny and Moe jumped out of nowhere from the top of the steps. I was practically shaking as I held onto the banister to catch myself while Benton was wide-eyed, trying to catch his breath.

Donny grabbed my hand and helped me up as Moe laughed.

"Sorry to scare you there," she giggled. "We were just heading to lunch. You should join us." She patted my shoulder with a big grin on her face. She was like a child and viewed everything as one giant fun-fest. I'm pretty she's more laid back at home than when she's around other people.

Moe suddenly dotted her eyes over to Benton with an arched eyebrow. "*Sooo*, who's your friend?"

I choked. Luckily, Benton introduced himself to them, but he shyly rose his hand up for a quick wave before gripping the straps of his book bag.

Donny chuckled. "No need to be so nervous, Benny. Can I call you that by the way? '*Benny*'? Or even '*Ben*', if you'd like?"

Benton nodded. Donny continued. "I'm Donald, but thanks to Meagan you can now call me '*Donny*'." He looked at me for a brief second and winked. He then pointed over to Moe. "And that's my sister Morris."

"Call me 'Moe'." Moe extended her hand for a handshake. Benton cautiously shook her hand as if he was afraid she was going to bite him.

The four of us walked to the cafeteria together and as we're walking in, Donny suddenly gasped and pointed to the necklace Benton was wearing. "Dude! Isn't that the necklace from *Allegiance Society*?! The one that was given to Agron from the Vampiric Elites?"

Benton nodded and Donny started geeking out.

He reminded me of a little kid who would get excited whenever his parents took him to the toy store. It was adorable.

Moe rolled her eyes in annoyance. She locked her arm with mine and whispered in my ear, "Hopefully they'll geek themselves to death and we get the last of the tater tots."

Amen to that.

After I went up to the lunch line and got my food, Donny introduced me to the three other people who were sitting with us at our table. A brunette named Carmen Richardson, a boy with a lisp named Peter de la Cruz, and a boy with dark hair and a thick Irish accent named Christopher Duncan.

"Welcome to the funhouse, kid. You've been promoted," Donny joked as he scooted over to make room for me to sit next to him.

As I sat down with my tray of food, Peter asked me if I was interested in going to prom with anyone and I thought I was going to cough up my chocolate milk.

I literally met the dude like 5 minutes ago and he was already asking me about prom. I didn't know if he was asking me to prom or was just curious. Regardless, I couldn't find anything to say to him as a response.

Christopher reached over smacked him on the back of his head. Peter winched while holding his head. I heard that smack too. I could tell it hurt. Christopher had some force in that backhand.

"Not cool!" Peter scowled at Christopher while eating his food. "That actually hurt you friggin' duck-face."

Christopher rolled his eyes. "Then don't be a creep next time." He popped a tater tot into his mouth. "And watch who you call a *'duck-face'*, eh. Next time I'll pop your eyes out."

Donny laughed, raising his hand to speak before Peter said anything. "Nah, cut the guy a break, Chrissy." Donny then pulled Peter closer to him and ruffled his hair. Peter shoved Donny off him as Christopher's face turned bright red.

"Chill out Don!" huffed Peter, picking through his hair.

"Don't. Call me that!" Christopher barked in Donny's face.

Peter was then like, *"Oooo!"*, as if he was a little kid and Donny was now in trouble with a teacher.

Benton was laughing while covering his mouth so he didn't spit out his milk. Meanwhile, Carmen and Moe were shaking their heads, rolling their eyes in annoyance while eating their lunch. I heard them mutter, "Dumb boys", and they proceeded to eat.

Christopher whipped his head around to face Carmen and he smiled widely, pushing the front of his hair back and out of his face. "Don't be like that Car, you know you love us."

"Only thing I love are these tater tots." Carmen leaned forward and popped two tater tots into her mouth.

Donny snorted, "Okay, time for the lovebugs to have their moment. Let's clear out."

Christopher's face turned bright red, and Carmen just flipped Donny off, telling him to get his head out of the gutter.

I continued to eat my lunch in silence.

It was kind of entertaining.

After school, Donny and Moe offered to take me and Benton home since things were still rocky with Lincoln Freedman.

Benton was a little hesitant but I was all for it. But I guess the thought of possibly getting jumped made him think things over, and he eventually agreed to the ride.

The car ride home wasn't a quiet one. From Moe bombarding me and Benton with all types of questions to Donny blasting the radio, a lot was going on in one sitting. Benton was sitting next to me, staring out the window, not really paying any mind to anything.

How? I don't know.

Moe continued to question us, asking all sorts of random things: *"How long have you two known each other?"*, *"So Benton, what's your favorite anime?"*, *"So Meagan, you like Runaway Capsules?"*, and even, *"So what's y'all story?"*

That last question really caught me off guard because I didn't know what the heck she meant by that one.

What's y'all story?

Donny interrupted Moe's question spree and told her to turn around and to leave us alone. He sounded bitter but he was mostly annoyed. Moe eventually got the message and turned around with her arms folded like a little kid.

"You're such a pooper, Don, you know that?"

"*Oye!* Don't take that tone with me, Morris-Lina."

Moe stuck her tongue out at him. "Jerk."

"*Bruja perra.*"

Immediately, Moe whipped her head around and scowled at him, her nostrils flaring. Donny was doing the best in his ability to not laugh too much since he was still driving, but the look on her face was to die for.

Donny eventually dropped me and Benton off home, but Benton had to walk across the street over to his house. I offered to walk over with Benton to his house, but he insisted that it wasn't a big deal. We wished each other goodnight before heading into our homes.

Your Friend,

Meagan Wright

Lee,

Donny and I got into a little debate this morning during homeroom since he disagreed with the fact that Runaway Capsules was better than the band HAVOX. Even though HAVOX has been around since the '90s, claiming that they're better than Runaway Capsules is a load of bull.

Runaway Capsules connects with our generation and has redefined alternative rock *and* pop collectively. They released their first album two years ago and they've already won a dozen awards, including *Best Alternative Rock Album* and *Music Group of the Year*. I can't remember the last time HAVOX has won either one of those awards. Just saying.

Donny refused to admit that I was right, but he knew that I was right. He'd just say, "Yeah, sure, whatever you say, kid."

So prideful.

Even though he wasn't supposed to be in my homeroom classroom, my homeroom teacher, Mrs. Rojas, allowed him to stay since she tolerated him. Turns out, Mrs. Rojas used to be his history teacher during his junior year, and he would ace every single one of her tests.

Donny says it's because he's *"the King of Notetaking"*, and I'd agree. I've seen him take notes for our class with Mr. Enrique. He's very thorough.

Anyway, the only reason Donny and I got into the conversation about Runaway Capsules and HAVOX was because he was trying to find a song that would be a perfect fit for the tribute video he was assigned to make for the teachers from the senior class. The tribute video had to be done in time for the Annual Senior Assembly in April, and according to Donny, it was nowhere near finished. In fact, Donny wasn't too thrilled about having to be the one to put the whole thing together anyway.

"It was supposed to be Tiana Burgess, but she's out of town and our advisor needed someone to do it," he groaned, resting his chin on the desk. "I said I would help, but that was with getting pictures. I didn't know I had to take the pictures *and* get video footage *and* find the music *and* make the whole friggin' video."

I chuckled. He tried to look intimidating when he glared at me but I ended up laughing even more. Finally, he just gave up and slouched in the seat with his arms crossed over his chest like a pouty child.

Benton came into homeroom a few minutes after Mrs. Rojas took attendance and she marked him late. She kept her eyes on him as he took a seat next to me and Donny. Benton paid her no mind, but Mrs. Rojas called him out anyway. She was like, "I didn't see you there earlier Mr. Son, you just coming in?"

Benton sighed, practically glaring at her. There were triple bags under his eyes, his hair was unkempt and looked a bit tangled, and he was slouching. He was not in the mood. I'm talking: *Don't piss me off today or I'll cut you.* If looks could kill—geez.

But Benton did eventually respond. "There was a delay with the train. Sorry." His voice was low and he avoided eye contact with Mrs. Rojas as if he feared just by looking at her, he would turn to stone.

Donny suddenly inched closer to Benton and sighed, "Shame I can't give you a kiss to perk you up like they do in them fantasy tales, pretty boy."

Benton just scowled at Donny before silently putting his head down on the desk.

Donny took that as his cue to head out, leaving me alone with a grumpy Benton Son. I scooted a bit closer to Benton and I could hear him breathing. I then heard him mutter something under his breath as his head remained rested on the desk, buried in his arms.

"If you want a picture, you go ahead. I give you my consent."

Dammit.

I shook my head, telling him to get over himself. Benton just looked up at me with a look on his face that basically said: *Girl, please.*

Benton sat up and attempted to put his hair up in a bun, but it was a nightmare. His hair was so knotted and tangled, I was getting frustrated just from watching him struggle. I had enough and I offered to comb his hair and he looked at me, practically stunned.

He was like, "You can do my hair? Really?"

"Uh, yeah. Why else do you I think I offered?" I snorted.

I told him that I would just comb out the knots, and I took out my comb from my bookbag.

45

(I never leave the house without my comb or a headwrap just in case my hair turns into an electrical accident. I'll spend a solid twenty minutes pressing my hair. It'll look nice for five minutes, but the second I step outside, especially if it's real humid, it frizzes and my beautiful work turns into a hot mess. That's why I keep a comb on me at all times, and even a few twist-ties for when I decide to pull my hair back into a poofy ponytail. That's if I'm not in the mood to braid it up. But today, I had to braid my hair in the girl's bathroom before homeroom and I covered my braids with one of my mom's patterned headwraps. My hair is such a struggle.)

Anyway, as I combed Benton's hair, he started to tense up a little bit since a couple of other students were watching us. I told him to relax and to pay them no mind, but he still hated being watched. I didn't understand why people were staring in the first place. I offered Benton one of my earbuds and we both listened to some music to distract ourselves.

After homeroom, classes went by real quick and hardly felt like classes at all. They were actually enjoyable.

For math class, Mr. Enrique split the class up into two teams for some math quiz game that he came up with, and the winning team would earn five extra credit points on the next exam. Donny and I were on opposing teams, and unfortunately, my team lost. Donny went on a whole gloating-spree and wouldn't shut up about the fact that everyone on his team would get five extra credit points on the next exam, which he really didn't need since he aces almost every test.

But whatever. It is what it is.

46

On the plus side, though, he offered to take me to Chick-Pot-a-Roo after school and buy me a milkshake to make it up to me. He knew I was a sucker for a good milkshake from Chick-Pot-a-Roo. They have the best homemade milkshakes in the city. That's what they're known for anyway.

So, after school, Donny took me to Chick-Pot-a-Roo and I ordered myself a chunky chocolate-chip milkshake with whip-cream on top. Donny got himself a peppermint milkshake with whip-cream and graham crackers sprinkled on top. We had to drink our milkshakes inside the restaurant since Donny has a strict *"no eating or drinking in the car"* policy. It was his *"Golden Rule"*.

Honestly, I don't blame him.

If I had a car like Donny's, I wouldn't want anyone drinking or eating my car either. He treasures that car as if his life depends on it. Moe even said that he would wash and wax his car every chance he could.

"He'll wash it almost every weekend and give it a good wax. He treats that car as if it's his baby and never lets anyone touch it. Not even me. Thank God he hasn't named it yet."

(The day Donald Gonzalez names his car is the day I will no longer be acquainted with Donald Gonzalez.)

While Donny and I sat in Chick-Pot-a-Roo, I received an email from the Philadelphia School District. Apparently, I was entered into the Annual Writers' Competition by the Philadelphia School District per request by one of my teachers.

I'll bet you a dollar that Mr. Rover was responsible for this.

Whenever he reads one of my papers, he always tells me that I have so much potential and that I'll be a well-known writer someday.

Still, I was anxious. It's not like a school writing competition. It's branched out to the entire school district, meaning students from other schools within Philadelphia could participate.

My nerves were starting to spike.

My nails are now numb from how much I was biting them. I always bite my nails when I'm anxious, and I know it's unsanitary but I can't help it. I either bite my nails or pick my lips, and my mom goes bananas when she sees me pick my lips.

So, I'd rather bite my nails than pick my lips. Although, that didn't settle too well for Donny as he drove me home.

The second Donny pulled up to my house, he clicked off the radio and looked at me. He said, "Don't pull no BS on me right now, kid. What's been bothering ya? You've bitten your nails thin. If I gotta deck someone I'll do it, just give me a name."

He was serious. I could see the fire in his eyes, he was ready to go on a manhunt. As sweet as that would've been, I didn't want that to happen. It wasn't necessary. So, I told him about the email I received from the school district about me being entered into the writing competition, and what does he do? He laughs. No, in fact, he was wheezing. Wheezing like a kettle. He stopped when he caught me glaring at him, and then he smiled like a bashful idiot.

"It's not funny, Donny," I told him. I slouched in the seat.

From the corner of my eyes, I saw him shaking his fists in the air, groaning. He snapped his finger in my face to get me to look at him and I flinched.

"*Oye! Chica!* Don't be like that now," he said, his voice getting a bit louder by the minute. He shifted his body around to face me completely and winced when his hip hit the steering wheel. I asked him if he was alright, but he just continued his speech on why I should stop being so worried since he believed that I would win the writing contest. "Meagan, I've seen your writings. You're pretty damn good. Trust me, kid, I'd bet my car on you."

He did in fact say that he would bet his car on me winning this contest. That meant a lot coming from him since he made it clear that you never mess with a dude's car.

"The most important rule is that you never mess with a dude's car. Especially not mine, so, with me saying that, just know I mean what I say."

I wasn't overwhelmed, I was just...*flattered*, you could say.

"Thanks," I told him. He lightly punched my arm, keeping a smirk on his face that sort of made me chuckle. "I'll take your word for it. The guy who never has any worries."

Donny snorted, his eyes wide. "Real cute, kid."

"Am I wrong? You seem to have things under control."

"Not everything. I got my doubts too, you know?"

He started telling me about this girl from his biology class named Mary Walsh. She sits three rows away from him towards the front. She has blue hair that usually wears in a single-braid, freckles, and hazel eyes that reminded him of a warm sunset. (Such a poetic visual.)

So, to make a long story short, he was thinking about asking her to prom but he was a little hesitant since he's never actually had a full-blown conversation with her that didn't involve classwork. The more he talked about her, his eyes lit up and it was clear that he was smitten.

It's a shame that a guy like him doesn't realize that he'd make anyone's day. He's epic. He had nothing to worry about and I told him that, but he was like me—anxiety tops confidence.

But then, Donny hatched up a clever way to solve both of our problems. A simple wager of encouragement: *I'll submit something for the writing contest and he'll ask Mary Walsh to prom.*

Solid deal, no backing out.

I told him, "A'ight, bet", and I shook his hand.

He chuckled. "*Sí*, bet."

As I was getting out of the car, Donny said to me, "Looking forward to seeing you with that first prize certificate, *chica*."

I reached through the window to give him a fist bump. "And look forward to seeing those pics of you and Mary Walsh on prom night."

He winked, clicking his tongue. I may not know what I'm going to write about for the contest, but a bet's a bet.

God help me.

Your Friend,

Meagan Wright

Section 2
2012-2013

Lee,

A lot has happened since the last time I emailed you.

Last week, I submitted my short story for the Philadelphia School District's Annual Writers' Competition, and when I told my mom, she was thrilled. She was like, "God's gonna make it work baby. I believe in you."

I also let Donny know that I upheld my end of the bargain. So now, it was his turn to jump into the battlefield.

Right after first period this morning, we hid behind the corner of the hallway as Mary Walsh made her way to her locker. I popped the collar of Donny's uniform shirt and dusted off his leather jacket. He kept watching Mary as she switched out her books and he turned his attention back to me. He croaked, "She's busy, I'll do it later. Cross my heart."

I grabbed him by his shoulders and stared him down. "Donald Esteban Gonzalez, you are a '*Gonzalez*'. A '*Gonzalez*' never backs down from a challenge, you said it yourself. If you solve impossible math equations, you can do this." I sounded like a drill sergeant.

Donny blatantly responded, "My middle name isn't '*Esteban*'."

"Whatever. Pull your head out the gutter and get your date."

"Alright, alright. Chill, I'm going."

And that's just what he did. He took a deep breath, blessed himself, and marched over to Mary Walsh and asked her to prom. I remained behind the wall, watching everything unfold. At first, it all seemed good. Note that I said: "*at first*."

I've never seen a person turn down someone so quickly without batting an eyelash. All I heard was Mary give Donny a harsh, *"No!"*, and she walked away. Donny watched her leave and I went over to him. I wanted to remind him that it could've been worse, but let's be real, that's a lie.

But Donny took things like a champ. Kind of.

He was a little flustered but hid it with his smile while making witty, random comments. He then threw his arm on my shoulder and suggested for us to go to Kenny's Dine-n-Dash after school.

"A squad hang after school. What do you say? They got the best waffle fries in good ol' Philly."

He wasn't lying. The waffle fries from Kenny's Dine-n-Dash are to die for, especially when you dip them in the soft-served crème shakes.

Before I could even say anything, he patted my shoulder with a big grin on his face and was like, "Good! See ya then, kid!", and he walked off.

The next time I saw Donny was after school as planned. Neither him or Moe were at lunch earlier since they were scheduled for counseling with Counselor Rashad and Counselor Malik. Benton told me during lunch that he also signed up for counseling, but he starts next week with Counselor Rashad.

"I heard he's pretty good," Benton said.

He suddenly asked me if I've ever received counseling from the school, and I told him that I did, but it wasn't for anything serious. It was my mom's idea, of course, and Principal Vickins thought it would help me manage my social anxiety in order to *"become a more well-rounded student and individual."*

I thought that I was fine, especially since you and I were going through things together. (In case you forgot, we made it through the Sugar Wars last year. Not many sophomores can say that they managed to survive their freshman year without getting bombarded with pounds of sugar and flour by the junior class. I remember the amount of time we spent mapping out what parts of the school we had to avoid. Sweet Jesus.)

After school, we all went to Kenny's Dine-n-Dash— me, Donny, Benton, Moe, Carmen, Christopher, and Peter.

To everyone's surprise, except for mine, it was Benton's first time going to Kenny's Dine-n-Dash, so he didn't know what exactly to order. He was tempted to order some fries while the rest of us had ordered crème shakes, but Moe managed to convince him otherwise.

But she was so dramatic about it, though. She had her hand on her chest and pretended to die, crying out things in Spanish. People were starting to look over at our table and Donny nudged her, telling her to sit up and to pipe it down. She sat up and made it clear that she could honestly care less about the people looking over at us.

Moe insisted for Benton to try the chocolate crème shake since it was *"much richer than the vanilla or mint"*. Blasphemy.

Benton looked over at me, wondering if he should go for it.

I told him, "I say go for it", and shrugged my shoulders.

Benton sighed. "Okay. One chocolate ice cream."

Moe clapped. "Now we're cooking, team." She threw her arm

around Benton and his body stiffened. Did she care? Of course not, but she wasn't being creepy about it. "And bud, it's '*crème shake*'. Get it right, partner." She was loud.

Donny hissed, telling her to shut up and to use her inside voice. He did that a couple times, actually. Donny would tell her to either lower her voice or to shut up, and in retaliation, Moe would laugh, calling Donny a "*party-pooper*". Donny's face would get red each time. I was afraid that he'd end up snapping and something would've gone down in the middle of the restaurant.

At one point, Christopher leaned over to Moe and softly asked her something with a concerned expression on his face.

Moe rolled her eyes and told Christopher, "Stop being such a dad, Chris." She then looked at all of us, beaming as if she had won the lottery. "Now. If you sissies are done lounging around, we're burning evening-light." You would've thought the girl had fifteen things of crème shakes with how bubbly she was acting.

As we were leaving, Moe and Carmen started talking about prom and tried to drag me into the conversation. No way I was interested in prom, I don't even think I'm allowed to go since I'm only a sophomore. But I guess if a junior or senior asked me, then I could go, but I doubt it. Plus, I have no interest in going.

Carmen snorted. "Prom is every girl's dream. Well, that and her wedding day."

I rolled my eyes, sighing. "Maybe for my senior year."

We were halfway across the parking lot when some random dude bumped into me. He looked back at me for a brief second but he continued on his way. Moe stopped and she asked me, "Did he apologize to you?"

I told her it wasn't a big deal but she was like, "Nah, manners. Look at him in his high-water tights. Some people." She tightened her fist and I reached for her hand, telling her to let it go but she slipped out of my grasp.

I wanted to follow her as she hurried over to catch up with the man but my legs were frozen. I called out to Donny. He looked back at me as he was taking out his car keys from his jacket pocket. He walked up to me and watched as Moe caught up with the guy, tapping his shoulder. The guy turned around and looked at Moe.

"Can I help you?" he asked, brusquely.

"You bumped into my friend, sir." Moe matched his tone.

The guy shrugged his shoulders. "Okay?"

Moe scoffed, completely irate. "Who do you think you are?"

That's when Donny finally rushed over, apologizing to the man as he tried to guide Moe away from the man. The look of embarrassment and shame on Donny's face was unbearable. The man kept shaking his head, a spiteful smirk on his face. The man could've just walked away like nothing had happened, but instead, he goes, "You beaners sure do get a kick out of meddling in other people's business, huh?"

In a hot millisecond, the man was on the ground with his hand over his face while Donny struggled to pry Moe away from the man. The hard punch sounded like something out of a movie, and when the man sat up, his mouth was bleeding. Lucky for him, he was able to scurry into the restaurant as Donny used all his strength to haul Moe away from the guy.

Donny had eventually let her go once they were near his car, and he went off on Moe. Her fists remained tightly closed by her side and I honestly thought she was going to swing at him, her own brother. Instead, she flipped him off and Donny's face was redder than a red balloon. He gestured for her to get in the car, and after an intense staring contest that felt like an eternity, she finally did.

Benton and I were the only ones who rode with them.

Carmen and Peter rode home with Christopher, even though Peter kept calling Christopher's car the *"Soccer-Mom Express"*. Christopher would flip Peter off and tell him that he was banned from the front seat. (I just think it was Christopher's way of finding a reason for Carmen to sit next to him in the front. It was obvious that he liked her from the way he would always stare at her.)

Anyhow, the ride home was dead silent. Donny didn't even turn on the radio which was torture. Clearly, he and Moe had reached a breaking point. They wouldn't look at each other. They didn't even attempt to acknowledge one another. It was just silent and unsettling.

I looked over at Benton a few times to make sure he was alright, but he just stared out the window. For a second I thought he had fallen asleep from how softly he was breathing, but he was wide awake. He was only staring out the window with a blank expression on his face.

I probably worry too much. It's something I'm trying to work on. I just pray to God that nothing like this happens again.

Your Friend,

Meagan Wright

Lee,

The only time I saw Donny today was during homeroom since he decided to come by and visit Mrs. Rojas. He also sat down with me and Benton for a bit, and we talked about the teaser trailer that was released last night for the new season of *Allegiance Society*. We were pumped.

Benton said that he hadn't seen the trailer yet, so Donny pulled it up for him on his phone. It was the most epic forty-seven seconds of Benton's life. His eyes were wide and his mouth was agape. Even though it was only a teaser trailer, we knew that the official trailer was going to be awesome. The new season was definitely going to make up for our displeasure with the way things ended last season.

"I can't believe we have to wait three damn months for the official trailer," Donny groaned.

Three months might not seem like a long time, but when it comes to *Allegiance Society*, three months feels like forever. Can you imagine how long we're going have to wait for the new season to premiere? We'll probably have to wait until the start of summer! It's torture. It's worth it, but it's still torturous.

Anyway, Donny had early dismissal after second period. Well, he *and* Moe had early dismissal, actually. I was on my way to my next class when I saw Moe gathering her things from her locker. I offered to help carry her things since her bookbag weighed nearly a ton, but she refused.

"I got it, thanks." She stormed off. I wanted to follow her, ask her what was up, but I figured she probably wasn't in the mood for any talking. She just seemed—I don't know—*out of it?*

During lunch, I tried not to think about Moe. I fought the urge to text her since I didn't want to seem clingy, but I couldn't get her out of my mind.

Carmen snapped me back into reality, asking me if I was planning on going to the Halloween party that was being hosted by one of the players from the hockey team. It's one of those parties where anyone can swing by, but there's going to be booze and a bunch of people there who I don't know.

Carmen pouted when I told her that I had plans. I really didn't. She whined, "You're such a wet-blanketed bore. What's it going to take to make you change your mind?" Christopher chimed in, snickering. "Maybe stop sounding like such a baby." He laughed at the scowl Carmen shot at him from across the table, and he adverted his eyes to me. "What if Donald went? Would that change your mind?"

I snorted. Even if Donny decided to go to the party, that didn't mean I would want to go. I'll be honest, since I've met him, I have grown a little bit more comfortable around him. That's the thing about him— he's like a force of nature once you get to know him.

Well, kind of. He's something. He just kind of grows on you.

You know that feeling you get when you hear a song for the first time? You're kind of skeptical about it, so you try to ignore it the best you can to get over it. But then, you hear it again, and again, and again— it just never stops. Then, after hearing the same song so many times, it starts to seem really catchy, and soon enough, you're humming along to the lyrics. You gradually start to realize how much of a thrill you feel whenever you hear the song, and eventually, you decide to add it to your playlist.

That's Donny, basically. I wasn't expecting to tolerate him for this long, but he's kind of grown on me a bit.

Anyway, the rest of my classes felt like a drag. I was ready to head home after sixth period but I still had to make it through seventh. When the final bell sounded, I quickly gathered my things and I was out the door.

While I was at my locker, Preston came up to me, and randomly asked, "Do I give off whorish vibes?"

I choked and my body stiffened. I shook my head, processing his words.

He could tell I was confused.

He then told me about his blind date with Jordan Q.'s co-worker. The guy was older by a couple years, and he was a sick perv. In summation, the hell-show of a date ended with Preston giving the guy a black-eye and a broken nose.

"I would've done better spending the night with a chipmunk than some sleaze who wears his trousers so far up his ass. He thinks I owe him some personal relief, which I can tell he gives himself every night while crying in the shower, listening to the blues."

Preston had every right to deck the guy. I thought it was surprising that he was telling me all this instead of Jordan Q. since she was the one who set them up.

Still, I let him talk and I listened. Before Preston had the chance to walk away, I answered his question and told him that he didn't give off any whorish vibes.

He looked at me with a deadpan face and replied, "I'll consider your input", and then he left. I groaned. He was always too complicated to understand.

On my way home, I decided to send Moe a text, asking if she was doing okay since she seemed a little off this morning. I was thinking of also sending a text to Donny to see how he was doing, but something in my gut was telling me to not even bother.

Moe hasn't responded back to my message yet but I doubt she'll respond now because it's almost 1 AM. With that being said, I need to get some sleep.

Your Friend,

Meagan Wright

Lee,

My Cousin Irene from New Jersey called my mom this morning to ask if we were planning on coming to the family reunion—on my father's side—this summer in July. There were many reasons why we didn't have to go and why we shouldn't go, but Cousin Irene was a good person. She always reaches out to us and asks how we're doing, which hardly ever crosses the minds of my other relatives. But, they were still family because I was still a Wright.

My mom confirmed with Cousin Irene that she and I would be attending the reunion. It was a bit of surprise that she'd even want to go. She and my dad were on good terms, but I could tell she still hasn't really moved on from him. I didn't know what to say in order to make her feel better.

Thankfully, Benton came over, unannounced, and the mood changed instantly. He knocked on the door and stood there, dressed in a polo with khaki slacks and his hair pulled up in a bun. I told him that he looked nice, and he smiled.

"Thank you," he replied, softly.

I stepped aside so he could come in.

My mom was in the kitchen, gulping down her second cup of green ice tea. She took notice of Benton as he stood in the living room, admiring the décor. She tossed the cup into the sink and walked into the living room and shook Benton's hand.

She never failed to show how fond she was of Benton. I bet she spends her nights praying to God that he and I will become a "thing", but that's not happening. Never. (Practically every girl at school thinks he's hot, and some guys are envious of his natural good looks.)

Benton only came over to say "hi", and I assumed it was Robyn's doing since she and my mom were now friends. I would sometimes see them talking to each other outside of their homes, sharing a few good laughs and having deep conversations. I was happy that my mom had a friend in the neighborhood, but she didn't have to think of a way for me and Benton to get closer.

The two of us were fine. Good friends.

My mom then suggested for me to show Benton around the house, which was stupid, but I did it anyway.

We went upstairs to my room and Benton looked around in amazement. He kept admiring the different posters I had on the walls and the shelves of books and action figures.

Benton suddenly took interest in the action figure I had of Lady McGaliga from the *Galactic Tracers Saga*. I was surprised that he's even heard of *Galactic Tracers* since people hardly ever talk about the series compared to *Allegiance Society*. But it's a fantastic manga series, ten volumes. I'm currently up to Vol. 6: *Taeki's Rebellion*.

"I remember spotting one of the books in the comic shop downtown, but I didn't really look into it until recently. It's pretty good." Benton kept his eyes on the action figure, smirking. "I'm guessing she's your favorite character?"

"Eh, Lady McGaliga is alright, but Avren Slater is my favorite." I stood beside Benton, keeping my eyes were on the action figure.

"McGaliga is the only one they made into an action figure, so I didn't have many options to choose from."

"You're kidding."

"I kid you not."

"Damn." He looked back at the action figure. "Can't believe it's *that* underappreciated."

"I know right! It's only ten volumes and it's one heck of a series at that."

I noticed Benton's eyes widen and he pursed his lips. "*Ten?!* I'm on the first one!" The first volume is the longest one in the series, as far as I know.

Benton and I spent a good amount of time talking about other books, manga, and shows that caught our interests. Like the novel series *Hannigan's Ball,* and the anime show *Instruments of Artemis.*

We were both disappointed with how *Instruments of Artemis* had ended since there were only two seasons and a third season would've given the show justice. Instead, the show ended on a ridiculously, completely unnecessary cliffhanger.

Thank God *Allegiance Society* didn't suffer the same fate. Then again, too many people love *Allegiance Society* anyway, so I doubt there's a chance it'll ever get canceled.

Benton didn't stay over for much longer since his mom called him on the phone, and he told me that he had to head back home for dinner. I walked with him downstairs and he wished my mom a goodnight before heading out the door.

He turned back to face me. "Team Pluto all the way?" It's a *Galactic Tracers* reference. (There are four different squadron fleets that are part of the Major Space Unit: Saturn, Pluto, Venus, and Mercury. Benton and I are both team Pluto all the way since they have the best recruits, one of them being Avren Slater, who's friggin' incredible!)

I placed my right hand over my chest and held up two fingers with my left hand. I cleared my throat and recited the Noble Vow. (Another *Galactic Tracers* reference.) "I swear on the stars of our ancestors that direct us onward to infinity."

Benton snorted with a faint grin on his face before turning on his heels to head back over to his house. I chuckled and closed the door shut. My mom popped out of nowhere, asking me all sorts of questions. Things like: *what did you and Benton talk about? Is he coming back over any time soon? Why didn't you ask him to stay for dinner?*

Too many questions, but it's my mother, so no surprise. I just answered her honestly before going back upstairs to my room. I then sat on my bed and decided to continue reading the rest of *Taeki's Rebellion* until it was midnight.

Your Friend,

Meagan Wright

P.S.— Moe just texted me. Her grandmother was admitted into the hospital a couple days ago after having a heart attack, which explains why Moe's been so down lately.

Lee,

My mom took me out for breakfast this morning to celebrate my birthday. To be honest, I've been so exhausted that I kind of forgot it was my birthday. It's strange since turning sixteen is apparently a huge deal, especially in my case.

Although, my mom was a little extra this morning with the early-morning celebration. I had finished taking a shower and when I entered my room, she was standing there with a giant balloon and a giant stuffed teddy bear and yelled out, "HAPPY BIRTHDAY MY COCOA PUFF!" The entire neighborhood probably heard her, not to mention, she scared the crap out of me.

At first, the lights were off, and when I came back into my room and clicked them on, all I heard was, "HAPPY BIRTHDAY MY COCOA PUFF!!" No warning whatsoever. I was afraid I would've dropped my towel, but thankfully, I have great reflexes. But even if I had dropped my towel, my mom wouldn't have cared. This is the same woman who will waltz herself into the bathroom without knocking, and she'll brush her teeth and wash her face as if I'm not even there. Anytime I had something to say about it, she'd always give me the same three responses:

1. *"I'm your mother, I've seen it all"*

2. *"Do you know how many times I had to wash ya behind?"*

3. *"You'd always rip your diapers off and run around naked in the house, so don't even."*

(The third statement is her favorite one since she'd always remind me of how much time she and dad would spend chasing me around the house to put some clothes on me.)

Still, I thanked her for everything. I heard my phone buzz on my desk and when I took a glance at it, I saw that my dad had left me a voicemail. Once mom left, I listened to dad's voicemail and I sent him a text, thanking him for the birthday wishes. I then got dressed and pulled my braids back into a long ponytail.

Mom decided to take me to one of my favorite diners, which was in a little town outside of Philadelphia. Mama Dee's Kitchen. The food was made from scratch and was always on-point. When we pulled up to the diner, I begged my mom not to tell them it was my birthday since I wanted a nice, quiet birthday breakfast. No singing or clapping.

She didn't listen. A bunch of employees came over to our table as we were eating and started singing and clapping. Then, everyone else joined in and it was so awkward. The singing was painful, I couldn't stand it.

I got a couple of text messages from Peter, Christopher, Carmen, and Benton—all of them wishing me a happy birthday.

Peter sent me a flood of GIFs with the words, **HAPPY BIRTHDAY**, shining bright, and Carmen sent me a couple of pictures of shirtless, hot guys as my *"birthday present"* from her to me. (I don't understand how the two of them don't have their own show on television.) Then there's Benton and Christopher. Both just individually messaged me a simple message: **Happy birthday**.

Once everyone stopped singing and left our table, mom

reached for my hands from across the table and we prayed silently. It felt as though I had held my breath for a solid minute until she finally opened her eyes and was smiling at me. She told me, "I remember when those doctors told me that you weren't going to make it past fourteen. Now look at you. Sixteen and counting."

It's true.

I've been living with my heart condition, Prolonged QT, since birth and I've had multiple surgeries. When I was eight, I had gone into cardiac arrest while I was at school and I was rushed straight to the hospital. The doctors told my mom that I wouldn't make it past fourteen. But under the grace of God, I was able to receive my Implantable Cardiovascular Defibrillator, and it does a better job at keeping my heart in check than my old pacemakers.

Since then, I've been fine. I have to take a few medications to help with my heart rate, but I'm still able to function like a normal person. Sometimes. I'd be lying if I didn't say that I'm truly blessed. So many times I could've clocked out of this world, but God was like: *No, no, no! Hold the phone! Not today!*

My mom says that I'm meant to do great things. I think that's something we're all born to do, you know? Do something great. But it's never easy trying to uphold that duty since it can be anything. I usually try not to think about it too much, but it gets hard sometimes because I'm always curious to find out what I can do versus what I can't do. Donny thinks it pays to be a little a curious at times, though. I guess he's right. A bit.

Your Friend,

Meagan Wright

Lee,

I was supposed to email you a few days ago, but I've been so busy working with Preston on our art project that Mr. Bissonnette assigned us. The project is due mid-February, but still.

Mr. Bissonnette is having the class work with assigned partners to create our own stop-motion short film. Mr. Bissonnette made it clear that the film had to be an original product and needed to reach the maximum time limit, which was ten minutes.

"I have seen many stop-motion films, and they are doable. No copying old material, I'll know if you do." He was stern and eyed us all down to the pit of our souls.

As I said, Preston and I are partners which wasn't much of a surprise since we literally sit next to each other in class. Plus, we work well together. Plus, Mr. Bissonnette has seen us work together before for theater last year. Preston and I would rehearse with each other and we'd even help each other with our costumes. I honestly wouldn't have wanted to partner with anyone else.

So, yeah. I've been busy with that lately.

Aside from all that, I've been wanting to tell you what happened on the night of my birthday. So, I got a text message from Donny around eleven-something at night and I was bushed. He sent me things like:

- **guess who's out here kid!**

- **U not asleep r u?**

- **it's freezing, plz wake up!**

I looked out my window and almost fell out my bed when I saw his face pressed up against the glass on the other side of my window. He was laughing hysterically and I was ready to clock him in the eye. He could've warned me or something, like: *Hey Meagan, I'm sitting outside your window. Don't wanna possibly give you a heart attack or freak you out.*

That sure would've been nice, but nope.

Still, I let him crawl through my window and into my room. He sat next to me on my bed and had the nerve to ask me how I was doing with a cheeky smirk on his face. I was still a little flustered and I just looked at him. "Are you joking?"

And he was like, "What?", acting all innocent. He shrugged his shoulders. "Not my fault you're such a scaredy-cat. I'll remember that for next time."

"You just caught me off guard is all. That doesn't make me a scaredy-cat." I was still trying to calm my heart down as I took a deep breath and relaxed back into my bed.

"Riiiight," he drawled with an arched eyebrow as he cocked his head to the side. "Well, until you learn how to not be so uptight, consider this as my apology." That's when he pulled out a small box from the pocket of his jacket and placed it on my lap. "*Feliz cumpleaños, chica.*"

When I looked at him, his honey-brown eyes lit up as if he were a child, and I noticed the light shade of redness on his cheeks. He was probably nervous that I wouldn't like his gift, or maybe his body was starting to warm up since he was finally out of the cold outdoors.

He was practically hovering over me as I flipped open the small box. I suddenly forgot how to breathe and my mouth was agape. I held the silver bracelet in my hand, admiring the little charms that were attached and dangled along the body of the bracelet.

Donny helped me put it on my wrist since it had one of those tiny clasps that were a pain in the butt to unlock and close through the ring on the bracelet. But Donny's like a ninja. He can do possibly anything without breaking a sweat.

I took a closer look at the charms. Donny said that they were all significant and were a reflection of me. In a way.

A Holy Cross because of my strong faith in the Lord, a book because I'm a book junkie, a pencil to represent my passion for writing, and then, a car that sort of looked similar to a Cadillac.

"I'm guessing the car is supposed to be you, huh?" I chuckled, turning my attention to Donny as a warm smile curled on his lips.

"Well, actually, it's supposed to be *us*. You can't deny that the gang and I haven't rubbed off on you in some way, right?" He leaned against me, chuckling at the end.

I nodded. "Seems significant to me, in that case."

For a moment, I thought of hugging him but my body just wouldn't cave in to the idea. I sat there, thinking of how to react to this perfect moment. A normal person with a pea-sized brain would've just said, *"thank you"*, and yet, I had the audacity to ask him, "How's your grandma?"

What a terrible way to show my thanks. I wanted to go inside my head, punch my brain, close up my head and then slap my face.

I watched as Donny's smile started to vanish as his eyes shifted away from mine. I figured I had crossed the line.

I tried to tell him that I was sorry because I had no right to mention his grandmother. It's bad enough that they're worried about her since she's so sick. Then I just had to bring it up and ruin the moment.

Donny was shaking his head, telling me that it was alright.

When he sat up, he turned his body so he could fully face me. I felt myself shrink as I started to lean against him. His arm was suddenly around me and he pulled me into his chest. I laid still, listening to his heartbeat as he opened up to me about his grandmother. He told me that she technically raised him and Moe when they were young since their parents were working all the time. Their grandmother would always stress the importance of getting an education in order to get ahead.

"She'd always tell me how much she wanted me to get out of here, move to bigger places, and do bigger things. She wanted the same for Moe too, and I know that's what our parents also wanted. But my *abuela* would always make it more clear than anyone else that's all she wanted for us."

He then told me about his worries for Moe ever since the incident at Kenny's Dine-n-Dash. He shifted his body a little bit to get comfortable and he pulled me in a little tighter.

He whispered, "You have to promise me that you won't go out and say anything about what I'm gonna tell you, alright?"

I looked him in the eyes and gave him my word.

Donny continued on, telling me that not too long ago, Moe had been diagnosed with bipolar. Their parents have done all they can to make sure she's properly medicated and goes to therapy, but sometimes, Moe isn't always compliant. Donny would find her medications completely untouched and he'd see the effects from it.

"Sometimes she's in bed literally all day and won't even come out her room. Other times, she'll walk around, not talk to any of us. The look on her face, it's as if she just came back from the slaughterhouse or was stuck in some cult against her will." He took in a quick quivering breath and held his breath for only a second.

I reached for his hand and clutched it tightly. I felt goosebumps awaken on my arms from the coldness of his hands. Donny blinked, letting out another sharp breath, telling me that he was okay. I wanted to believe him, I really did, but his eyes said a different story.

I threw my arm over his waist to hold him a bit. I said to him, "I got you", and I meant it.

His smirk widened a bit. "I got you always too, kid." He sighed, rubbing my back. "Still like your gift though?"

I snorted out a chuckle. "Duh."

I wore that bracelet for the next couple of days, including today. Today was the first day Donny actually had the chance to see me wear the bracelet since he and Moe were actually at lunch today. Moe kept begging Donny to take her to the Halloween party that everyone's been talking about. He tried not to pay her any mind but she eventually got on his nerves, and finally, he agreed.

Well, he actually said, "Fine, whatever. Jesus."

Of course she was happy about it. She started smiling and

73

wrapped her arms around his neck. She even gave him a kiss on the cheek and ruffled his short hair. He flinched, telling her to ease up and to not mess up his hair.

Meanwhile, Benton and I were stuck at home being good, nerdy scholars while everyone else decided to party all night. I really don't do parties, it's just not my thing. I don't think it's much of Benton's thing either.

Your Friend,

Meagan Wright

Lee,

Mr. Rover decided to do things a little differently for the start of class. Instead of going over last night's vocabulary worksheet, he told us a personal story about the time he tried to pull a prank on his parents. (It didn't relate at all with our lesson. He just told us to tell us.)

He said he was eight-years-old at the time and he had filled in his little brother on the prank, which was stupid. The prank was also horrible, a total set-up for something to go down. It involved him stealing his parents' credit cards and hiding them in the freezer. The prank totally went south since his little brother ratted him out, and as the saying goes: *snitches get stitches.* So, Mr. Rover clocked the hell out of his little brother, which led to him getting, what he described as, *"the worst beating known to man"* from both parents.

Majority of the students in the class were cracking up, while the rest sat in absolute disbelief. In the beginning, I was a little shocked but his facial expressions cracked me up as he was telling the story. (This is why Mr. Rover will forever be the best teacher to walk the streets of North Philly.)

Still, after that, Mr. Rover reviewed last night's homework, and then he had us work on some grammar practice sheets during the rest of class. When it came time for my art class, Donny sent me a text message, asking if I wanted to come over to his place to go over our practice sheet for our math class. I immediately responded back with a thumbs up to let him know that I was up for it.

Preston then came into art class with a beanie on his head and a bruise on his cheek. When I asked him what had happened, he scowled at me and told me that it wasn't a big deal.

"I fell, alright?" He was lying. His eyebrow twitches when he lies—that's his tell.

I nodded my head, not wanting to cause a scene. I just told him to be careful next time, even though I still didn't believe him. We spent our class time in silence, listening to Mr. Bissonnette's instructions regarding the short stop-motion film project.

When our class ended, I asked Preston if he would mind me walking him to his next class period. He looked at me with a strange look on his face, it's sort of hard to describe. Maybe he was baffled that I even offered, I guess. But all he said was, "I'm fine. Don't worry about it", and then he was gone.

He probably ran into some punks from our school who were trying to start something with him. Knowing Preston, he probably didn't feed into their nonsense, and so, they decked him. But it could've also been his mom. She's always lashing out at him, hitting him for no reason—just out of pure spite and resentment.

I remember Preston telling me that after he came out to his family, his father had killed himself and his mother blamed him for everything. She even tried to get his brothers to turn against him, but that didn't work out so well for her.

Preston didn't deserve that, no one did.

When I got to the cafeteria, I noticed that Moe and Donny weren't there. They were probably attending one of their counseling sessions again. I saw Christopher standing at the end of the line for the vending machine and I snuck up behind him. When I poked his cheek, he nearly jumped out of his skin and looked at me with wide eyes.

"S-S-Sorry," I chuckled. "I thought you were a tough-guy."

Christopher rolled his eyes and ran his fingers through the front of his hair. "Knock it off, will ya?" He let me stand beside him as he waited in line. "You want anything?"

"No thanks," I told him. "I'm surprised you're not trying to snag a spot in the lunch line next to Carmen."

Christopher quickly shifted his attention to me, his mouth open as if he was going to retaliate and speak but no words came out. He finally gave up and sighed, looking down at his shoes.

I snorted. "Come on, it's a joke."

"Well, don't joke like that anymore, alright?" He wasn't mad, he just sounded sad. He was like a little kid that just lost his favorite toy in the world with no hope on getting it back. He shook his head, letting out a sigh. "Sorry, I'm fine."

Lies. Anytime someone acts like that and then says they're fine, they're not fine. I ought to know. That's my go-to whenever someone asks me if I'm fine.

I shook my head.

"No, I'm sorry," I said to him as I rested my head on his shoulder. He chuckled and patted the side of my head. "But seriously though, do you have a thing for her?"

That wasn't even a question. It was obvious he did.

It was finally Christopher's turn at the machine and he noticed no one else was behind us. He let out a sigh as he inserted the coins in his hand into the machine and selected a bag of chips. I stood there with my hands in my pockets and he looked at me with his face turning pale. He nodded his head, saying, "I do. Yeah."

I lightly brushed my fist against his shoulder. "Alright now, I see you!"

Christopher's face was bright pink. "Cut it out," he muttered.

We moved over to the side so we were standing in the corner of the cafeteria, practically out of sight. The way his eyebrows furrowed showed how cautious he was about everything.

He started fidgeting as he told me about his feelings for Carmen. It was adorable. Turns out, he's liked Carmen ever since they became friends their sophomore year. He's tried to get over it multiple times since she's been interested in different guys and she would always go to him for advice. But her crushes never worked out in the end, and Christopher still believed he had a chance. Eventually, they started spending much more time together, and he wanted to confess his feelings to her, but he never had the guts.

But then came the night of the Halloween party.

While they were at the party, he had been contemplating on whether or not he should've asked her out. Peter was the one who encouraged Christopher to listen to the little voice in his head in order to figure out what to do. So he did, and he finally asked her out. But he did it after the party, which was smart. Although, her response was kind of unexpected.

Carmen didn't tell him *"yes"* or *"no"*.

According to him, her exact words were, *"I don't know"*.

Like, come on. It's obvious that she has feelings for him too. He's not the only one who acts smitten whenever they're together. I've seen the way she looks at Christopher from across the table sometimes, and how playful she gets around him. All of us can tell that they like each other.

Christopher's face went pale again as he popped open the chip bag and leaned against the wall in distress. He mumbled something but I could hardly make out what he was saying since his Irish accent was so thick. But I let him know that it wasn't the end of the world. Besides, I've been in his position before—wanting someone who you're not sure wants you back, and it's so complicated that it makes your head hurt.

(Last year, there was a guy in my English class who I thought was great—his name was Peter. He and I would talk sometimes, but he was very complicated. Sometimes, he was open about his feelings, and other times, he was distant. I used to think it was a guy-thing, but it was actually just him. Nothing ever happened between us, though. We eventually fell out of touch.)

We've all been there at some point. But Carmen's response to Christopher's question threw him in a loop. It was killing him, I could tell.

I just told him, "Consider her saying *'I don't know'* as a comma rather than a period or a question mark. It'll give you both time to really think things over until you finally have that *'aha!'* moment.

Once you do, then you'll know what to do."

I tried not to sound too optimistic because I often jinx things when I get too optimistic. But Christopher didn't mind at all. He pulled me into his arms and patted me on the back.

"You really are an alright kid, aren't ya?"

"Did Donald tell you that I was?"

Christopher reached to touch my hair but I backed away before he had the chance. He started laughing when he saw that I was ready to fight, but luckily for him, he knew better. (You never mess with a girl's hair. Ever.)

As we were heading back to our lunch table, he promised that he would take my advice and said he was willing to wait for Carmen.

They would look nice together. Even Donny thinks so.

In fact, while I was over Donny's place after school, going over our math practice sheets, he said that he told Christopher a long time ago to ask Carmen out.

Donny was like, "I've been shipping them since the summer of our junior year. Like damn, feels like we're in a soap opera."

But at the end of the day, it wasn't really up to us to put them together. If we even tried to force it to happen, we'd never hear the end of it.

Your Friend,

Meagan Wright

SENT: November 5th, 2012

Lee,

Preston wasn't in class today and I should've known something was up since he takes perfect attendance very seriously. He then messaged me during class, asking if I could meet in the back room of the gym by the staircase. I responded to his message, letting him know that I would be on my way. I was able to excuse myself from class.

When I found Preston, he was leaning back against the wall, his face turned away from me in an attempt to hide his bloody, bruised face. When I lifted his chin, one of his eyes was completely shut while the other was watery. I could tell he had been crying because there was a stream of dried tears on his cheek, lightening the dried blood. His bottom lip was cut and when he would try to open his mouth, a soft noise would come out rather than words. His khaki pants were scuffed and there was blood on his Polo too.

I helped him up and we went into the back room so I could clean him up a bit. He kept holding his ribs and winced every time I pressed the damp towel against his face. All he could do was make noises, not words.

A million questions ran through my mind and I was set on calling up Donny to help me find the punk who did this to Preston. Telling the principal would've been the civil option, but Preston was in rough shape. He could hardly walk. The school would probably do nothing about it. I wanted whoever was responsible to pay for this, but then, Preston put his finger to his lips, indicating that he wanted me to keep quiet. I thought maybe taking the civil option would've been better then. I was so tempted to drag Preston down to the main office so he could fess up to Principal Vickins on who did this to him. But he wouldn't let me.

Every time I tried to convince him to say something, he'd shake his head, telling me to keep my mouth shut, otherwise, things would get worse for him. Him saying that gave me the idea that it probably had to be someone who messed with him before.

I remember last year, when someone spray-painted **FAGGOT** on his locker, and when he opened it, a bunch of syringes spilled out of his locker. The school never cracked down on who was responsible for the stunt, but I have a hunch it was them douchebags from the lacrosse team. But no one was going to rat on them, not a chance.

I helped Preston walk down to the nurse's office on the second floor. Once we got there, he asked me to wait with him until he was called to the back. I did exactly that. I asked him where he left his bookbag so I could run and get it for him. He said he managed to get in his locker before he got jumped.

"I had finished my meeting with Dexter and I put my bookbag away since I didn't feel like lugging it around today. I was just going to take out whatever I needed if I had to, but then they grabbed me and dragged me into the gym and…well…yeah." His hand started shaking and he was looking down at the ground. I reached for his hand to settle his nerves and he let out a quivering breath, shifting his attention to me. "You can't say anything,

Meagan. You got that? This gets out…they'll…they…" For the first time ever, I saw fear in Preston's eyes. He had to look away from me for a second to get himself together but I still had my hand over his.

I wrapped my arm around him and pulled him close so his body was resting against mine. He was light. Shoot, he probably weighed no more than 150 or 160 pounds. If he wasn't so tall, I could probably give him a piggyback ride.

Anyway, I didn't want to crush Preston's hand so I loosened my grip a little and I assured him that I wouldn't tell anyone.

He did have a point though. If someone did end up finding out about things, it could get worse for him. Especially if the guys from the lacrosse team did have something to do with this. They're merciless assholes. Not all of them, but some of them.

Once Preston was called into the nurse's office, he told me to head back to class. He said he would be fine but I honestly didn't want to go back. But I had to listen to him, it wasn't up for debate.

Mr. Bissonnette called me out for being out of class for more than fifteen minutes and I had to think of an excuse to get him off my back. "My mom called me. It was a family emergency, really. You can check my call history if you don't believe me."

He huffed and just told me to take a seat and to finish working on my mosaic.

The rest of the day, I kept thinking about Preston. I figured the nurse allowed him to be dismissed early since I didn't see him at all for the rest of the day. I texted him during lunch, asking if he made it home okay but he never responded back.

Benton tapped on my arm and asked if I was okay since I was a bit in a daze. I tried to think of something to say, but no words came to mind. All I could do was nod and look away again.

Out of nowhere, Moe leans across the table and she asked me, "So, going to prom or naw?" She just had to start that conversation up again.

Moe was amused by the look on my face and she sat back down, nudging Carmen. "I told you she would get like that. I told you," Moe cackled. Carmen rolled her eyes and slipped a dollar bill in Moe's hand. Moe dramatically sniffed the dollar before stuffing it into her pants pocket. "I'm gonna make a fortune off of placing bets with you, Car."

"Keep dreaming, Morris-Lina. This time was just a fluke." Carmen shot a glare at me. "You owe me a dollar girlfriend." She smirked.

All of a sudden, you'll never guess who came over to our table to speak with me. Nathan Hendricks. We were all looking at each other like, *is he lost or something?*, and then, he started talking to me.

He even said my name. I was surprised he even remembered my name. He didn't say much, though. He only apologized for messing with me earlier in the year, saying it was a stupid dare that he was pressured by his friends and Diana into doing. He then looked over at Donny and held his glance. Nathan kept opening his mouth, trying to find the right words to say but he never could. He just closed his lips and shifted his glance back to me.

I could tell Nathan meant every word he said to me. I still don't know what made him have the balls to come over to our lunch table. I figured it was probably because Diana wasn't in school today and that's what Donny assumed as well. Christopher thought that maybe there was a possibility that Nathan was trying to be decent for once.

Donny laughed at the idea. "Really? Quit playing, Chris."

Christopher sighed. "Think about it," he said. "Don't forget that before Diana, it was the three of us, Don."

I almost choked on my orange juice. Benton patted my back, asking if I was alright. I was fine but I couldn't believe that once upon a time, Nathan and Donny were friends. I always thought they hated each other's guts. Donny shot an icy glare at Christopher that could've turned the boy into stone. Everyone at the table was quiet and Christopher didn't see anything wrong with his statement. He just kept staring back at Donny, absolutely unintimidated.

Finally, Donny took a sharp breath and turned his attention back down to the food on his tray. I heard him say to Christopher, "Go to hell."

Christopher shrugged nonchalantly. "Only if you go with me."

That sort of decreased the tension since Donny looked up at Christopher for a bit and smirked. Christopher looked over at Peter and nudged him on the side.

"What're ya pouting for?" he snickered.

Peter whined like a child, "I hate when you two fight."

Christopher ruffled Peter's hair which was something he really shouldn't have done since Peter was about ready to kill Christopher for messing up his look. Christopher knew what he was in for, so he sprinted up out of his seat and Peter chased him through the cafeteria like a man on a mission. Too bad Christopher had longer legs and was much faster than him. Peter could never keep up.

After school, Benton and I went over to Donny and Moe's place to sort of hang out, although we spent most of the time studying. But once we were done studying, Moe thought it would be a good idea for us to play truth or dare. Donny thought it was a stupid idea but Benton and I were down for it. So, we played.

Every time it was Benton's turn, he picked truth since he was very anxious about the possible dares Moe would make him do. Eventually, Moe groaned, telling Benton to pick a dare and she gave him her word that she wouldn't make him do anything out of pocket. He was hesitant but he did eventually agree to do a dare. It was nothing crazy, like, she didn't make him kiss a stranger or something. She dared him to text his crush and his face flushed.

"I-I-uh-I-I, I can't." He was so embarrassed. Moe thought he was trying to chicken out but he shook his head. "No, no, no. I just…don't like anyone…right now."

Moe still wasn't convinced. "A fine boy like you, I don't buy it. There's gotta be someone you like."

Benton fell silent. Donny saw how out of place Benton felt and he lightly bumped his shoulder against Benton's to get his attention. He told Benton that it wasn't a big deal and that he would text his crush instead so Benton wouldn't have to worry about it. Benton opened his mouth to oppose but Donny didn't care. I already knew who he was going to message.

Mary Walsh. All he did was text her: **hey.**

Donny showed Moe his phone and she rolled her eyes.

"Now I get why you spend so much time in the bathroom," she snickered. Donny plucked her on the forehead and she winced, rubbing her head. *"Diablo!"*

Donny turned his focus over to me. It was my turn to pick someone. I picked Donny. He chose to tell the truth. I didn't know what to ask him. Some things I already knew the answers to, so it would've been dumb to ask them. Still, I had to ask him something, but what I asked him was pretty stupid.

"Is it true what Chris said at lunch about you and Nathan? Were you guys...friends?"

It was so quiet. Even Moe was baffled by the question. Still, he nodded his head and answered, "Yeah, it's true", but that was all. He could hardly look at me.

Then Benton spoke up. "What happened?"

Donny looked up when Benton asked. Donny shifted around on the couch and leaned forward, letting out a sigh. He had a faint smile on his face but the look in his eyes was tough to make out—hurt, maybe?

All he said was, "Diana happened", and no one thought to ask a follow-up question. I wouldn't have guessed that he and Nathan were once buddy-buddy, and I wouldn't have guessed that he would still feel hurt about whatever happened between them. I could tell he was hurt, he just wouldn't admit it.

Moe was the one who decided to call it a night. Donny took me and Benton home but before I got out the car, Donny grabbed my hand. I was a little confused.

In a hushed voice, he told me, "Thanks for today".

I pressed my lips together in a tight smile.

I know it doesn't seem like much but it meant a lot to me. For some reason, he thanked me for whatever reason. I guess today felt different for him.

Honestly, I should've thanked Donny for making the rest of the day feel alright. In fact, every day with him feels alright. I guess that's why he's one of my favorite people. I hope he knows that by now.

Your Friend,

Meagan Wright

Section 3
2012-2013

Lee,

Benton invited me over to a family gathering going on at his house this evening, and my mom insisted on me to go. I didn't have a choice. I had to go. I was skeptical because I didn't know anything about his extended family, but I also didn't want to face the wrath of my mom either.

My mom ironed my plain gray dress for me to wear with my black dress shoes. I only applied a light amount of make-up to cover my dark spots, and I wore my hair half-up, half-down.

I was heading for the door and here goes my mom, "You look so cute, let me take a picture!"

It's not the first time she's seen me look like this, but I let her take a couple pictures so I didn't have to hear about it later.

I finally went over to Benton's house. There were so many cars parked outside their house and I could hear some music playing from their backyard. When Robyn answered the door, she pulled me in for a hug and welcomed me into her home.

Once she closed the door, she called for everyone's attention and spoke to them in Korean while standing by my side. Everyone was now looking at me and I felt queasy. I still smiled and politely said, "Hello". Some people said, "hello", and others just nodded with straight looks on their faces.

I felt out of place. Not just because I was the only chocolate chip in the room, but everyone was dressed so nice and I felt ridiculously underdressed.

Seeing Benton didn't make me feel any better. He looked sharp. Real sharp. His hair was pulled back, making it easier for me to his defined cheekbones. He wore a dark blue blazer over his crisp white dress shirt, a pair of dress pants with matching dress shoes. It wasn't fair that he looked so good.

"You look nice," he said to me out of the blue.

"Thanks," I told him. "So do you."

He chuckled. "Thank my mom for that." He stared at me for a second. "I like your hair. You look beautiful."

"Thanks." My throat was starting to get a little dry. "You look beautiful too." *I'm such a dumbass.*

Benton chuckled, rocking on his heels.

His father, Han, eventually called him over and Benton excused himself. I looked around at the different people around me, his relatives. I could feel some of them eyeing me, but I knew it wasn't out of admiration. The dryness in my throat thickened and my palms were starting to sweat. I had to get out of there.

I decided to sit outside on the porch to get some air. I felt my stomach tightening in knots as I sat down on the porch step. I had my head in my hands, sighing. It's not that being over there was a mistake, it's just the staring that really got to me. So sitting outside was the best I could do for myself.

As I sat outside, someone came up behind me and I nearly jumped out of my skin. It was one of Benton's older cousins, and he cackled like a hyena when he had startled me. He said that he didn't mean to scare me, but that was hard to believe since he got such a kick out of it. He introduced himself as Avery and he extended his hand for me to shake. He was older than Benton by a couple years, and he kept his hair short and had big hazel eyes.

I introduced myself to him. "Meagan," I said, shaking his hand. Avery's eyes widened. He assumed that I was Benton's girlfriend but I shut that down real quick, telling him that Benton and I were only friends.

Avery chuckled. "I'm only teasing, I'm only teasing." He loosened his tie as he sat down beside me. "You and my cousin are one of the same. You can't take a joke."

I could so take a joke. I'm friends with Donald Gonzalez for crying out loud, the king of jokes. Jokes and sarcasm.

Anyway, Avery told me that Benton had told him a lot about me and that he was already aware of our friendship. He just wanted to mess with me for a good laugh. He also said that he was pretty glad that Benton and I were friends since it's usually hard for Benton to befriend anybody.

"Benton and I grew up together for a bit before he and his family moved from place to place. He would never come home happy, always so miserable. He only talked to me or Roselle, but he'd sometimes keep to himself. He'd get picked on a lot but he wouldn't say anything to his parents. He'd just get more and more miserable every day. So I thank the Heavens that he met you."

I gulped. It's no wonder Benton seemed so stand-offish when we first met. I'd be stand-offish too if I always came home after a long day at school and was being constantly picked on for no reason. It was pretty sad.

Avery cleared his throat and decided to change the subject since he felt as though he was killing the mood. He started talking about himself but not in a boastful way. He told me that he was in his third year of college as a nursing student at Frankford Hollands University in Georgia. His father didn't like the idea of him being a nurse, but Avery basically said "*eff it*" and went into nursing.

Respect.

He then told me about his girlfriend, Chloe, who he had met during his first year of college, but they didn't start dating until last year. He showed me her picture on his phone and my gosh, she was pretty. She was a brunette with rosy cheeks, blue eyes, and a dimpled smile. I was like, "Whoa", and Avery was like, "Told you so."

He went on about how she was an advocate for social justice and was an active member of an organization on their campus that promoted awareness for global warming. He spoke out of admiration and thrill, gazing out into the open space. He was in-love. I was waiting for the hearts to form in his eyes.

"She's crazy too. She has so many big ideas that seem impossible, but she does all she can to defy the odds." He kept smiling and started nodding his head. "I think I'm going to marry her one of these days."

And he meant that too.

Avery was ready to head back inside, but then he turned back around asked me, "You like my cousin? Benton?"

I practically fumbled with my words. "Well—we're friends."

Avery laughed. "Yeah," he nodded. "You changed him."

"How?"

"He smiles more." With that, Avery waltzed back inside the house. I stayed outside, not wanting to take the chance of having all eyes on me again.

Benton soon came outside and sat beside me. Being the gentleman that he is, he apologized for leaving me alone but I told him that I was fine. When I told him that I spoke with his cousin Avery, his eyes went bonkers like he was about to flip out. He started apologizing, saying that Avery was a mad-man and didn't mean anything crazy that he said.

Benton held his head. "Sorry about him, I swear."

I snickered. "We were fine, Benton. Really."

"He can be a bit much sometimes," Benton said, looking down at his shoes. He seemed a bit embarrassed and I noticed his cheeks starting to flush. "Mind if I walk you home?"

I asked him, "The party's over?"

He nodded.

I took him up on his offer and he smiled as we crossed the street over to my house. We wished each other goodnight and then Benton wrapped his arms around me and hugged me.

Benton Son hugged me. I was not expecting that at all.

I hugged him back though.

"See you at school?" he asked.

I nodded. "See you at school, Benton Son."

A smile curled on his lips and I watched as he headed back over to his house. I walked into my house and saw my mom sitting on the couch, watching TV. She asked how things went over at Benton's, and I told her that everything was fine. She took my word for it. She then scooted over so I could sit next to her as we watched old TV shows from the '80s.

Your Friend,

Meagan Wright

Lee,

I had a cardiology appointment this morning and learned that my defibrillator needed a new battery, which means I am going to have another surgery. I can't stand being hooked up to machines and staying in a hospital bed with an IV in my arm. The IV makes my skin itch sometimes, it's annoying.

Still, I had to just suck it up and deal with it. Everything was out of my control. Fortunately, Dr. Tami and Dr. Viktor would always make sure I was properly taken care of and would check up on me whenever they had the chance. Dr. Tami and Dr. Viktor have been my cardiologists since I was a baby, so I trusted them with everything. So did my mom.

They said that they were going to arrange for my surgery to be early next year but they would call us to confirm a date. I was fine with that, but I knew that I would end up missing a couple of days of school because of it.

On the car ride home, my phone was blowing up with a bunch of text messages from my friends. They were all wondering why I wasn't in school and I felt bad for not telling them about my appointment. I never missed a day of school. They were very aware of how serious I was when it came to having perfect attendance. So missing a day of school was a little unsettling to them, I guess.

At least when Donny and Moe miss a few days of school, we're all informed on why. Well, Donny will often inform Christopher, and then Christopher informs the rest of us.

My mom sighed. "I bet your friends missed you today?"

I nodded. "A little bit." More like a lot.

I could've easily messaged them in a single group text and told them everything, but in the back of my mind, I knew they would have a ton of questions. Still, another part of my mind knew that I couldn't completely leave them in the dark. It wasn't fair.

I was often teased in grade school because of my heart condition, same for middle school—but high school? So far, high school has been something different. It's been a bit more settled. Like, no one really cares unless they're told to care. So that's probably a little easier to deal with compared to grade school and middle school.

So, without another thought, I messaged them all in one group message and told them about my cardiology appointment, and I explained to them about my heart condition. I felt my thumb twitch as I hit SEND. My chest tightened and I rested my head back against the headrest. My heart was pounding so hard in my chest, I thought it was bound to burst.

When we got home, I felt my phone buzzing in my pocket and I looked at the text messages from the group chat. A ball formed in my throat as I read their messages. Christopher said that he had a cousin back in Ireland who has the same condition that I have, and he told me to stay positive.

Peter sent a GIF of a baby wearing shades with the caption

YOU GO GIRL.

Carmen sent about a million hearts and smiley faced emojis and messaged: **You're awesome! Love you! Stay strong!**.

Benton sent me a really long message, privately, saying that he supported me and that he thought I was brave. Moe did the same thing. She sent me a private message and told me that I was strong and that she believed in me.

I didn't hear from Donny 'til dinner time came around. His message was nothing long, but it really did put a smile on my face.

- **You're going to be alright, kid.**

I knew he meant it too. They all meant everything they had said, I knew that for a fact. I could only imagine what they'd say if I had to tell them about my surgery. (It's just a thought. I'm not planning on bringing that up any time soon. I still have time.)

Your Friend,

Meagan Wright

P.S.— I got a text message from Preston a few minutes ago, by the way. He's doing fine. He said that he was staying over Jordan Q.'s house for a couple of days, but he didn't explain why. He didn't have to

Lee,

I was in homeroom when I received an email from the superintendent of the Philadelphia School District, informing me that I was one of the finalists in the writing contest. The email included the date and time of the Annual Writer's Banquet, which was going to be held at the Hillman Banquet Hall near Penn's Landing.

I forwarded the email to my mom and about five minutes later, I got a text message from her, telling me that she was extremely proud of me. I sent her a smiley face as my response.

I then asked Mrs. Rojas if I could be excused to the restroom and she tiredly handed me—tossed me—the hall pass. The pass slipped out of my hands and I could hear Mrs. Rojas chuckling as she held her head in her hands. I didn't pay her any mind as I grabbed the pass and darted out the door.

As I was on my way to the bathroom, I felt someone practically jump on my back and I shrieked. I turned around and saw Peter laughing his head off like a donkey.

I huffed. "You're sick, you know that?!"

Peter lifted up his hands defensively and shook his head, a smirk plastered on his face as if he was innocent. "Hey, just take the joke." I heard a smack and Peter was holding the back of his head, wincing.

Christopher stepped forward from behind him while shaking his head. With a deadpan face, he told Peter, "Sometimes I wonder if God even questions your existence." A little harsh, I think.

Peter snorted, throwing his arm around Christopher. "Oh Chrissy, if I had to look up a blundering asshole, I'm sure you'd come up on my search engine real quick." Peter lightly tapped Christopher's chest, earning himself a scowl from Christopher.

I sometimes wonder how the two of them can even tolerate each other. I know it's all fun and games, but I'm sure to a point, they probably mean half the things they say to each other—calling each other *"assholes"* and whatnot. It didn't seem to mess with their heads though. Like, they would never get angry at each other, or start huffing and puffing.

Plus, to be honest, Christopher was like the wise owl of the group and that was something Peter sort of admired.

Anyway, I could tell the boys probably forgot that I was standing there because they kept going back and forth with each other for a solid minute or two. I cleared my throat to get their attention and they snapped out of their little banter.

Christopher cleared his throat and asked me if I had any plans after school. I told him, "No", and he and Peter exchanged glances. I asked them, "Wassup?", and Peter started fumbling with his words. I could hardly make out what the heck he was trying to say.

Christopher rolled his eyes, probably thinking Peter was the biggest idiot on the face of this Earth. He then chimed in. "After school we're going over to my place. I wanted to surprise Don with something, and wanted to know if you would want to join us. You in?" Christopher spoke with such authority, his voice actually sounded a little deeper than normal.

I asked them, "What's the surprise?"

Peter managed to get himself together and he arched an eyebrow, looking at Christopher for approval to speak. Christopher gestured his hand forward, basically giving Peter the go-ahead to talk. This felt like a privilege to Peter because his eyes lit up like a firefly's bottom and he spoke with so much enthusiasm. More than usual.

"We're giving him a pitching machine, you know, for baseball. Chris's dad used to play and Chris is too much of a dweeb to play, so." That last comment earned him a hard punch to the arm.

Christopher explained to me that Donny used to play for the school's baseball team up until his junior year, which sent everyone into a spiral since Donny was one of the best players on the team. (Actually, Donny was probably the best player alone, according to Christopher. He said that almost everyone in the school thought that Donny would one day be recruited by a scout to play for one of the best colleges and eventually land a spot in the Major Leagues.)

So, when Christopher found out that his dad was planning on selling his old pitching machine, he immediately thought of Donny and knew it would be the perfect gift for him. I just couldn't get over the fact that I never realized that Donny used to play for the school's baseball team.

Then again, I hardly had any time to attend any games last year to show school spirit. But it seems like every day I'm learning more and more about the many wonders of Donald Gonzalez.

I gave Christopher my word that I would keep the pitching

machine on the down-low. Christopher then asked me if I could find out if Benton was able to come over to his place after school.

He wasn't. Benton told me that he had to go straight home after school since his grandmother was planning on visiting his family since she wasn't able to attend their last family gathering.

I didn't see Donny this morning for math class, but I did see him after my second period class, and he didn't look so good. There were dark circles under his eyes and fresh redness in his eyes. I noticed dried streaks stained on his cheeks from where he must've been crying, and his cheeks were completely flushed.

When he said, "Hey", his voice sounded shaky.

I felt my chest tighten and I tried to think of the right things to say. "You sick?" I asked him.

He told me, "Nah." He cleared his throat and sniffed.

"Then what's the matter with you, and don't say it's nothing."

To tell you the truth, it was kind of scary seeing Donny like this. Well, not *scary* but it sure as hell wasn't an easy sight. He then told me about his grandmother. She died last night in her sleep, he said. He predicted that it was only a matter of time since the doctors said she was getting worse, but he didn't want it to happen.

Donny started wiping his face again but he wasn't crying.

"You want a hug?"

Donny shook his head, adjusting the straps to his book bag. "You're such a sap, kid, you know that?" A cheeky smirk curled on his face, and he threw his arm around me as we started walking to the stairway. "What class you got next?"

"Art," I told him. "You?"

"P.E.," he sighed. "Mind if I walk you to your class?"

"Isn't it out of the way for you?"

He shrugged. "I could use the calorie burn."

Donny was in perfect shape already. He'll often joke about how much he liked to eat and that he was a total pig, but in reality, Donny was in the best shape out of all the guys. Sometimes I would notice the sleeves of his leather jacket showing off his muscles a bit.

When we finally reached my art class, I told Donny that I would see him at lunch. He said he would be there. He was about to walk away and I called out to him before he had the chance to make his way to the staircase.

I asked him if he was going over Christopher's house after school and he nodded. "I was just talking to Chris, he knows I'll be over," he said. "Are you going?"

I nodded. "Yeah."

He curled his lips and winked, clicking his tongue. He then bounced down the steps to get to his next class. I found myself smiling as I entered the classroom and sat in my usual seat next to Preston, who looked like a zombie from complete exhaustion. I tried not to look at him for most of the period though. I took little glances at him, just to see if he had any fresh bruises or cuts since things haven't been going so well for him at home.

He seemed fine though.

We just spent most of our time in class strategizing what we should focus on for our short film project. It was actually coming together quite well. We decided to make a short film about a boy wandering in the park, looking for his toy train, and while he's looking for his toy train, he encounters different beasts that offer him advice on staying hopeful. (I was surprised that Preston liked the idea.)

After school, I met up with Christopher and he immediately started to question me, wondering if Donny was still in the dark about the pitching machine. It was kind of insulting that he'd think I'd slip up and ruin things for him. I told him that I kept my mouth shut about the whole thing. A sigh of relief came from him.

I could tell this was huge to Christopher.

I thought maybe this had something to do with Donny's grandmother dying. Maybe this was Christopher's way of cheering him up or something. Or maybe he was just doing it because he cared *that* much for Donny.

The two of them were like brothers. If something went down, they'd call each other first before reaching out to anyone else. They looked out for each other as if their lives depended on it. Even when it came to Peter. Peter was like their little brother—someone they had to look after. Not because he was incompetent at taking care of himself, they were just super protective of him.

Carmen once told me that Donny almost got into a fight with one of the guys from the hockey team since the guy kept making fun of Peter's lisp. Christopher had to convince Donny to walk away because he knew that if Donny had done anything, Donny would face the consequences by the school, not the other guy.

It's sad but true.

Anyway, I rode with Donny to get to Christopher's place, and when he pulled up to the house, I felt my jaw drop to the ground.

Christopher's house was beautiful.

He lived in a nice suburban area but none of the houses looked the same. Some were big, some were small, but none of them were average. They all stood out somehow. Christopher's house was the most captivating. It was a nice two-story home but the inside was bigger than expected. There like three bathrooms, four bedrooms, the kitchen was super nice and modern, so was the living room. The backyard was breathtaking. It was big enough to build a small-home, or two, and was surrounded by oak trees.

Donny threw his jacket on the lawn chair outside in the backyard and wiped his forehead with the back of his hand. "Damn, is mother nature losing her head today? It feels like eighty degrees out here," he huffed, fanning himself.

"I know right," I sighed.

Carmen came up behind Donny and she poked his side. He turned around, completely unfazed by her presence. She then motioned for us to step aside as Christopher and Peter wheeled out a large machine, covered by a thick blanket. I glanced at Donny as he stood there, watching as Peter and Christopher lifted the machine off the hand-truck.

Christopher wasted no time ripping the blanket off the machine and once he did, Donny's jaw dropped and his face lit up like a candle.

"Duuuude," Donny gasped. He took small steps forward, completely mesmerized by the shiny pitching machine. It was in great condition, looked practically new. "Isn't this your dad's?"

Christopher shrugged his shoulders, a smug look plastered on his face. "It *was* my dad's," Christopher said, taking a few steps closer to Donny. He just kept his eyes on Donny and his smile was wider each second.

Donny was confused at first, but then, it clicked. He practically leaped into Christopher's arms, almost knocking them both down but they managed to catch themselves and stood tall.

"S-S-Surprise!" Christopher chuckled.

Donny had the biggest smile on his face, bigger than a child's on Christmas morning. It was like nothing I had seen before. Peter came up from behind Donny and threw his arm around his neck.

"And for the first time ever, Donald Gonzalez has been stunned! Tell us how you feel?" Peter pretended to hold up an imaginary microphone to Donny, keeping his arm still locked around Donny's neck.

Donny snorted and said something to Peter in Spanish that made Peter shove him. Peter muttered in Spanish and Donny cocked an eyebrow, snickering. He turned his attention back over to the machine and threw his arm around Christopher.

As I was looking on, Carmen stood next to me and had a twisted grin on her face. When she stepped into the sunlight, I noticed all the little freckles on her face and the shine on her forehead from her oily skin.

Even without make-up, she was like a little doll.

I turned my attention back to the boys as Christopher started to load up the machine with a few baseballs.

Carmen leaned over towards me and muttered, "Get ready to buckle up and witness one of the many wonders of Donald Gonzalez."

When the first baseball spat out from the machine, Donny took a swing and sent the ball flying to the far end of the yard, close to the trees. Each time a ball came his way, he managed to send it flying. I don't think he missed a single one.

He really could've gone pro. He would've if he hadn't quit.

Carmen told me the real reason why he left the baseball team.

Their junior year had been a rough one for Moe, Carmen said. Moe would sometimes have breakdowns and she'd shut people out. It tore Donny to pieces. He did all he could to make sure Moe was okay, and so, he thought it was best to quit. He quit for Moe.

I'm pretty sure if the roles were reversed, Moe would've done the same for Donny. You know the saying: *you do for family*.

Still, I could tell it broke Carmen's heart that Donny gave up one of his passions. It breaks my heart too. I'm sure his parents weren't too happy about it either since he could've earned some type of scholarship for college. But he's a smart guy, so I'm sure his grades will get him a scholarship somewhere too.

But it's obvious that Donny loves his sister to pieces.

Heck, she's the love of his life.

When it comes to the people he cares about, Donny thinks he's suddenly Agron Melhart from *Allegiance Society*— he tries to take on everyone's burdens as if they're his own, and he'll do all he can to take on the world.

It can be a scary thing to think about sometimes, you know? Having all that responsibility on your shoulders. It weighs you down into a bottomless pit, and the more you sink, the more you feel like you're going to break. I didn't want that for Donny, and I'm sure Moe doesn't want that for him either.

Your Friend,

Meagan Wright

Lee,

This morning as I was heading to homeroom, I spotted Nathan Hendricks outside of Dexter's office and he was signing up for the theater program. I honestly couldn't believe it. I didn't want to believe it, but it was true. My eyes weren't fooling me. Nathan actually signed up to be part of the theater program.

At first I thought it was probably for an assignment since taking part in the arts is a required class subject.

But then I was talking to Preston during art class and turns out, he and Nathan had a little chat about it before school had started. He said that Nathan had approached him and he started asking Preston all sorts of questions about joining theater. He seemed very interested, Preston said.

All of a sudden Nathan Hendricks was turning over a new leaf.

First, he apologized to me the other day, and now, he's interested in being a part of the theater program. I figured he was probably losing his marbles. Turns out, according to Preston, Nathan and Diana had broken up the other day. Preston heard about the news from Jordan Q., and at first, everyone was stunned. Literally stunned because Nathan worshipped the ground Diana had walked on.

I remember asking Preston, "How did it even happen? Why did it happen? It doesn't make any sense."

Preston rolled his eyes and he told me that Nathan sort of

ended things with Diana after Nathan had found out she had been seeing one of the guys from the lacrosse team behind Nathan's back. Preston didn't know exactly who Diana was seeing, but he had a hunch that it was possibly Austin Brown since he and Diana had a history.

"Austin and Diana were on-and-off, kinda. They had been that way since freshman year, but then, Nathan came into the picture. Nathan was better for Diana anyway. But I guess Nathan could never meet her expectations in certain ways."

It's pretty stupid, to be honest. Giving up on someone because of little things, and then having the nerve to go back to a terrible ex-boyfriend. (Austin is the worst. I would see the way he'd treat other people, tearing them down and whatnot. It pisses me off that no one's thought of breaking his balls— maybe then he'd realize he's not so hot.)

Nathan was a good guy. Stupid but still good. But I guess he's trying to get himself together, now that they're over. It's not like he wanted to end things, but she technically cheated on him.

It's a bit sad.

Anyway, I saw Moe after my art class and she wasn't looking so hot either. She had her hair pulled back and I could see the dark circles under her eyes. She always had a bit of a round face, but for the first time, I could actually see her cheekbones. She didn't look normal. When I asked her if she was doing alright, she just nodded and told me that she was exhausted. Even when she spoke, her voice sounded drained of life.

She wasn't just tired. She was way past being *"just tired"*.

I asked her if she wanted to head up to the cafeteria together for lunch and she looked away from me. Her voice quivered as she gripped onto the straps of her bookbag, still avoiding my eyes. "I actually have an appointment with Counselor Malik, so I won't be at lunch," she said.

I felt a tightness in my chest. "Oh." I cleared my throat. "Well, I can walk up with you if you want. Just to make sure you get there alright, you know?"

She shook her head. "I'm good, thanks." And then she was gone. I watched as she darted up the steps to get to Counselor Malik's office. In my head, I kept telling myself to go after her. That's what a good, decent friend would do anyways. I knew something was up with her, and yet, I just let her slip away from me like it was nothing. I wanted to punch myself in the face.

But what could I possibly do for her? I doubt she'd even talk to me and tell me what's really bothering her. The only person she'd really open up to is Donny. Not the counselors, not Christopher, not Carmen or Peter, not even her parents. It always comes down to Donny— probably the one person who actually gets her.

Maybe it's a twin-thing? Better yet, it's probably just their thing.

I was still thinking about Moe during lunch. I didn't want to seem like the clingy friend, but I knew I shouldn't have just let her run off the way she did.

I could've at least made an effort to talk to her. I mean, yeah, I did, but I could've done more.

I could've asked her if she needed anything or something.

I just didn't like seeing her the way I saw her.

She was not herself at all. It was frightening a bit. But I had to stop thinking about it and accept that there was nothing I could've probably said or done to get her to talk to me.

I suddenly felt Donny tap my shoulder, and when I looked at him, he cocked his head to the side, motioning for me to follow him. He didn't say anything until we were alone in the back end of the hallway. He sat down on the floor with his head rested back against the wall.

I sat by him with my knees pulled in as he asked me, "Did you see Morris-Lina this morning?"

My throat was dry and I felt my heart starting to race. He looked at me with a deadpan face and his jaw tight. What really caught me off guard was him saying her full first name. Usually he just refers to her as 'Morris' not 'Morris-Lina'.

I gulped. "Only for a second or two."

"How was she?" he asked, this time he was looking at me.

I shrugged. "Alright, I guess." Lies. I honestly don't know why I lied. Maybe I just didn't want him to worry about her too much?

Donny scoffed and crossed his arms over his chest. He asked me upfront, "Are you lying to me?", and I felt ashamed for even trying to pull one over him.

I chewed on my lips, not knowing how to respond. I was probably giving myself away by turning away from him, but what could I really say? I didn't want him to worry himself to death. After all, Moe did still go to counseling. That's good enough, right? I mean, I probably should've been upfront with him since that was his sister, but I know how Donny gets.

He gets upset. Very upset. He'll often beat himself up about things he can't control and it's not right. I didn't want him to beat himself up about this. And yet, I couldn't even look at him.

I couldn't look him in the eyes and tell him how I really felt.

I couldn't even look at him when he offered me his jacket, insisting that I was probably cold since I was shivering. I didn't even know that I was shivering. I just felt his arms come around me and my back rested against him.

Donny let out a quivering sigh. "You still cold, kid?"

I shook my head. "No."

I allowed my body to relax against his and he hooked one of his arms across my stomach. I rested my head against his chest, hearing the soft rhythms of his heartbeat. I started remembering the night he came into my room on the night of my birthday. He had pulled me in close to him just like this right before opening up to me about his grandmother and Moe. I remember his face as he was telling me about Moe's diagnosis and how much she mattered to him. I could tell how much she mattered to him—he didn't even have to tell me.

We just stayed like that for a bit, Donny and I.

Something in my gut was telling me that the others were probably wondering where we were since the bell was going to sound at any minute, signaling the end of our lunch period. Yet, as I was ready to get up, Donny's arms tightened around me, pulling me back against him. His breathing was shaky and his hands felt cold.

I managed to get a good look at him as I shifted my body

around while lying in his arms. He had his head rested back against the wall and he opened his eyes. They were glossy, as if he was on the verge of tears but was doing everything in his will to not cry. Asking him what was on his mind would've probably made me seem invasive, so I just asked him if he was okay but that was no better. Donny snorted and started to sit up, his hold around me loosening up. But then he froze. His eyes were fixed on me and his lips were parted. I was waiting for him to say something but each time he opened his mouth to speak, he'd close it shut.

Finally, I asked him, "What's with you? You can talk to me."

He sighed, running his hand down his face. He made me swear to not say anything to anyone and I felt my chest tighten. I still gave him my word, but I knew that whatever he was going to tell me, it must've been serious. I sure was right.

His eyes never left mine and he leaned forward as he spoke to me. His voice quivered. "There's this center in Texas that specializes in mental care, and my parents told Morris-Lina about it the other night. She didn't really take it all too well but it's the best for her. It's pretty far but they'll do all sorts of things that'll help her. I read about 'em."

For a second, I forgot how to breathe and I felt my heart suddenly drop into the pit of my stomach. *Moe...in Texas?* I understood that they wanted her to have the best care possible, but Texas was far. Very far. It's not like it's an hour-something drive to get there from Philly.

I could only imagine Moe's reaction when her parents sat her down and told her that they were sending her away to some rehabilitation center in Texas. She probably flipped. I would've too.

I asked him, "How long would she be there for?"

He responded, "We're not sure. It could be for a long time."

A ball started to form in my throat and my heart was racing as if it were in a marathon. I sighed, resting my head back against the wall. I didn't know what to say. What did he even want me to say?

He said that the only other person within our friend group who knew about everything besides me was Christopher.

I'm sure Christopher was just as baffled as I was when Donny told him the news.

Can you imagine what that'll do to Moe? Being away from Donny for God knows how long while being in a different state? It'll ruin her. They should know better, him and their parents. There are probably places in Philly that'll be better for her anyway. But Donny said that their minds were set, and when he told Christopher, things didn't go so well.

He didn't talk about it too much, what happened between him and Christopher, but I can only imagine how the conversation went down. Words were probably exchanged and Christopher probably questioned Donny's judgment once he found out the whole thing was Donny's idea. (Oh yeah, Donny told me that it was his idea to send Moe away. So you can imagine what was going through my mind when he told me that it was all him and not his parents. I couldn't even say anything to him because I was afraid of saying the wrong thing.)

I wanted to tell Donny that the whole thing was a bad idea. He and his parents should reconsider, but what kind of friend would I be to question him? Moe was his sister, not mine. But at the same time, she didn't really have much of a choice. The choices were being made for her and nothing good usually comes from that.

There's always another way. I know there has to be one. I just pray to God that I'm proven wrong. This is the one time I actually want my gut to be wrong.

Your Friend,

Meagan Wright

SENT: December 16th, 2012

Lee,

Carmen invited us to her little cousin's birthday party at Den &
Berry's, the best restaurant and arcade known to man. Even though
it was the weekend, I figured my mom wouldn't allow me to go
because she's overprotective and hasn't ever had the chance to
actually meet my friends, other than Benton.

Yet, to my surprise, she actually allowed me to go—on one
condition: she expected me to be dropped off before dinnertime.

I called Carmen yesterday, letting her know that I would be able
to go to the party, and she squealed.

"How'd you even get your mom to let you go?" she asked.

I shrugged. "Maybe she's warming up to y'all."

Carmen huffed. "About damn time. Although, that's a bad
idea." She snickered. Before I got off the phone, she insisted for
me to wear my best outfit since pictures would be taken.

(I was praying to God I'd be left out of them, but knowing
Carmen, she'd probably drag me over to get in the shot.)

So, today I wore my favorite V-neck blue dress with the thin
straps and the hem draped over my thighs. I did my make-up and
curled my hair.

Mom insisted on taking a picture of me before we left but I was
worried about being late to the party. She rolled eyes, telling me it
wouldn't take long. I groaned. She took about five different photos

of me and I felt my anxiety spike as we were finally leaving the house.

As I was strapping myself in the front passenger's seat, I got a text message from Benton, telling me that he wouldn't be able to go to Carmen's little cousin's birthday party since Roselle was sick and he wanted to stay home to take care of her.

(I still don't think Roselle likes me very much, but I've come to the realization that it's probably because she's just overprotective of him. After what Benton's cousin, Avery, had told me—about Benton being teased when he was younger—it's no wonder Roselle acts the way she does whenever she sees me. She's probably just looking out for her little brother, I guess.)

I then got a text from Moe, alerting me that Carmen's looking for me. I felt my stomach starting to twist in knots as my mom finally pulled out of the driveway and started to drive down the street. Luckily, it didn't take us too long to get there—maybe about twenty minutes. Still, I hate being late.

I gave my mom a kiss on the cheek once she pulled up to the front entrance of Den & Berry's, and I practically sprinted out of the car. I called Carmen as I was heading inside, letting her know that I was there. She told me to meet her at the front of the arcade entrance, which I did. When I saw her, she looked as though she was about to drop and she had her face painted like a tiger.

I chuckled. "You look nice."

She rolled her eyes, taking my hand to guide me to where their family was situated. There were a bunch of kids and teenagers running around, playing arcade games. Adults were either sitting at their booths, talking, or getting drunk at the bar.

Carmen was saying something to me once we arrived at their section, but I could hardly make out what she was saying. It was something about a cake and presents. I saw Christopher sitting on a bench outside the booth section, playfully bouncing the baby he held in his hands on his lap. Meanwhile, Peter and Donny were playing around with a couple of little kids, letting them jump on their backs and roughhouse with them.

I felt someone stroke their fingers through the back of my hair and I jerked my head forward. When I looked behind me, Moe was snickering with her hand covering her smile. I told her through my teeth to never touch my hair, and she rolled her eyes.

"Yeah, yeah, yeah," she said, waving her hand. "We're just glad you finally made it, otherwise Carmen would've lost her shit."

Carmen elbowed Moe's side, making her wince as a faint chuckle escaped her lips. Carmen hissed something to Moe in Spanish and then whispered, "I got family here, be a little considerate of that, yeah?"

"Alright, alright, sorry," Moe groaned. "I'll be good."

Carmen gave Moe a side-eye glare with her lips pursed and arms folded across her chest.

Moe clicked her teeth and settled her hands on her hips.

One of Carmen's older cousins came up to her and asked if she could help with something. Carmen excused herself, and Moe asked me if we could take a quick stroll before it was time to cut the cake. I nodded.

We were on the other side of the arcade, a good distance away from the party. She was curious to know if Benton was showing up or not and I told her that he had to stay home to take care of Roselle.

"That's his sister, right?" she asked.

I nodded. "Yeah. She's older."

She dramatically batted her eyes, cooing out, "Awwww, such a sweethearrrrt".

I snorted and lightly nudged her in the arm, earning a laugh from her. I felt myself breathe a little easier when I saw her smile. It was definitely better to see her like this than when I saw her the other day at school. She looked alive this time—like herself.

I then started to feel nervous when I thought about her being sent away to some rehabilitation center in Texas. I didn't bring it up while I was with her, but the thought was hard to get out of my head. I was probably being selfish since it probably was the best for her, but I didn't want that to be the only option. And Lord knows how long she'll be there for. Not even Donny knows when she'll be let out—and the whole thing was his idea.

But he's only looking out for her. I know that, but still.

Moe and I took a seat on a bench that was between two arcade games. A couple of little kids were running around with tokens in their hands, heading to one of the machines across from where Moe and I were sitting.

Moe let out a sigh as she watched them. "I miss being that young," she said, softly chuckling.

I realized I was picking my lips and I smacked my hand, telling myself to stop. I knew I was nervous but I couldn't keep picking my lips. I wouldn't hear the end of it from my mom.

I heard Moe ask me if I was alright and my fingers started to feel tingly, as if they were being electrocuted. I looked her in the eyes and I could still see the circles under her eyes. They were lighter this time, though.

I cleared my throat, nodding my head. I fiddled with my fingers as my heart started to pound heavily in my chest. I had to take a couple deep breaths in order to make sure I didn't fall out. I knew it was all in my head—the anxiety from everything. I just had to keep telling myself to stop overthinking like I always do. I told myself to believe that things were going to be fine.

And I had to believe it. It'd be no good if I just didn't believe it.

I noticed Moe looking down at her shoes as she started talking. I can't remember everything she had said at first. The arcade was loud and too many people were passing by. I could hardly focus but I made sure that I didn't take my eyes off her.

She then leaned back, stuffing her hands into the pockets of her oversized hoodie and she crossed her legs. I heard her ask me, "Did Donald ever tell you about me? About my condition?"

I gulped. I had to play dumb. I knew what she was talking about, but I couldn't just throw Donny under the bus. I told her, "No", and she snorted.

She found it hard to believe. I don't know why but she did. "All the times you guys have been together, he ain't ever say anything to you about me being bipolar?"

My palms were sweating but I kept my hands clasped together

on my lap. I didn't say anything because I didn't want to slip up and make it obvious that I was lying. I just shook my head and she sighed. She didn't seem bothered, just a bit surprised. But the truth is, I did know about her being bipolar. I knew about her diagnosis and everything. But she still told me anyway because she didn't know what I knew.

The only difference was that she was a bit more open about it than Donny was when he told me.

Moe told me that she was in middle school when she was finally diagnosed, and she's has been in and out of therapy while receiving different medications to help treat her. For a while, her family had been trying to keep her diagnosis on the down-low, she said, but she figured it probably wasn't for her sake.

She looked down at her fingers and started picking at the skin. Her eyes were becoming glossy and she let out a quivering breath.

"My parents haven't really looked at me the same since. Then again, I don't think they viewed me any other way, now that I think about it. Mom's always been too tough, dad's always too soft. Funny thing is, they're not like that with Donald, they're both neutral with him. And Donald, he'll…" She pinched her eyes shut and let out a sharp breath. I pressed my lips together and scooted myself a little closer to her 'til my arm brushed against hers. Moe looked up with a faint grin forming on her face. "I just wanted a brother, not a caretaker." Her voice was shaky and I could see the tears forming in her eyes.

Her cheeks were flushed and she cleared her throat, holding back the tears as much as possible. Knots formed in my stomach and I felt a tug in my throat, as if I swallowed a pill and it was just stuck in my throat and wouldn't go down no matter how much water I drank.

I found myself shaking as I rested my hand on her back. Still, I had to let her know that through it all, Donny did love her. He did.

"He loves you is all," I assured her. I wanted her to know that she wasn't a burden.

I don't know what their parents are like, but I know Donny. I knew him well enough to let Moe know how he really felt. She was his whole world. He shows it in everything he does, even if it's not always done the best ways.

Moe snorted, tucking a strand of hair behind her ear. She sat with her legs slightly spread apart and her hands clasped together.

"Love is a complicated thing to want, depending on where it's coming from. I shouldn't have to worry whether or not if it's real or just pity, you know?"

Yeah—I did know. I used to think like that when I was younger. I used to think I was a burden on my parents. They would always worry about me because of my damn heart condition, I could never catch them a break. Sometimes I'd think about just leaving, relieving them of their troubles. But I could never do it. I pictured my mom crying and my dad hating himself.

So I stuck around a little longer. But soon, I realized that they did love me. Every time they said it, they'd show it. Even if they weren't together, they'd still take the time to show me how much they cared about me. I think that's the best thing, to be frank.

But Moe didn't get that. I don't know if she ever will.

I didn't want to give her false hope, tell her that things would get easier down the line because I didn't know what things were like in her shoes. But I still told her to have patience. That's something I had to learn for myself. Then things got easier. Maybe if she tried it, it'd get better for her. Eventually.

Moe and I didn't talk much after that. We went back to the party and made it back just in time as Carmen's aunt had started cutting the cake. Carmen's aunt gave her daughter the biggest slice since she was the birthday girl, although the piece was bigger than the girl's whole head.

I was offered a piece of cake but I only took a little slice since I wasn't really in the mood for cake. Christopher and Carmen were sitting together at their own booth, talking and laughing—being cute. Donny waltzed his way over to me and threw his arm on my shoulder.

Peter joined us, still stuffing his face with chocolate cake and getting little crumbs on his shirt like a child. Donny just looked at him, shaking his head. Peter shrugged his shoulders, arching an eyebrow.

"What?" he said, chewing on the thick piece of cake that was already in his mouth. "A Dominican's gotta eat."

"Like that though?" Donny questioned, pointing at the little crumbs on Peter's shirt. "You know your aunt would have a fit. The cake's not going anywhere, *hermano*."

Peter wrinkled his nose, mockingly imitating Donny's words while using his own napkin to dust off the crumbs from his shirt. I looked over and saw Moe standing off to the side, talking on the phone with someone. She hardly looked at any of us. Even when she came over to us, she hardly said a word.

Donny took me home and Moe sat in the front passenger's seat. No one said a word and Donny had the radio blasting to make up for the silence. When I entered the house, mom was in the kitchen, cooking dinner while on the phone with one of her co-workers, laughing. I went straight upstairs and I plopped down on my bed, thinking a bunch of *'what if's'* and *'how 'bout's'* on how everything with Moe would play out. It's a lot, sometimes.

Your Friend,

Meagan Wright

Lee,

My mom got the call yesterday from Dr. Viktor, informing us that my surgery would be on January 3rd, and that I would have to be checked into the hospital on January 2nd. Honestly, this whole thing blows because I really don't want to miss the first week back to school.

I went down to the principal's office this morning during homeroom and informed Principal Vickins about my surgery. She was very understanding and wished me the best.

I figured that after telling Principal Vickins about my surgery, it'd be best to let my friends know since I wouldn't be in school once winter break was over. The hard part was telling them about my heart condition, and now that that's over, it should've been a breeze telling them about my surgery. But actually finding a way to bring it up made things sort of complicated.

I couldn't just tell them out of nowhere, *"Hey guys, just so y'all know, I have a heart surgery at the start of next year, so I won't be in school for a bit, okay?"* It's not as easy as it seems, you know.

But I had to tell them, otherwise, they'd probably hate me for leaving them in the dark. I wouldn't hear the end of it.

I thought about telling them during lunch, but as soon as my art class had ended, Preston grabbed my hand and handed me a stack of flyers that advertised the interest meeting next week for the theater program.

"Dexter wants these up before the end of the day and I can't do all of them alone, so you're gonna help me." He then settled a stapler on top of the flyers in my hand.

You gotta be kidding me?! I asked him, "Why didn't you just ask Jordan Q. to help you? She's free isn't she?"

Preston shot me a glare and tightened his jaw. "She has music with Mister Kioshi. Now quit being such a putz and start stapling these on the bulletin boards. I'll cover the second and third floors, you get the fourth and fifth. Got it?" He gave me a side-eye glance as he took his stack of flyers from off the floor by his stool.

He was out the door so fast, I couldn't even get a final word in. If he weren't so tall, I'd probably put him in a headlock 'til he said '*uncle*'. He wasn't even asking for my help, he just dropped everything in my hands and told me to go do whatever he asked of me. But there's no fighting him on anything. That's just how he is, and yet, I haven't knocked him upside his head yet.

One day, I thought. One day.

I started on the fifth floor since I knew there was no way I was going to finish by the end of lunch since the staplers were a pain. My fifth period class was on the fifth floor anyway, so I could just head to class if I wasn't able to finish hanging up the flyers by the end of lunch.

Each time I stapled a flyer to the boards, the stapler would get stuck and I'd have to use all my strength to pry it off the board without ripping the flyer. I felt my hands starting to cramp and I eyed the stapler as it remained stuck on the board.

"Need some help?"

To my surprise, Nathan Hendricks was standing in my presence with a faint smile on his face and his eyes were on me. He reached over my shoulder and gave a gentle push to the stapler before gently pulling it off from the board. If only I had more upper-body strength, I would've taken that out with no problem.

When Nathan handed me the stapler, he asked why I didn't use push-pins since it would've been easier. As if I hadn't known that already. Push-pins would've been better but I understood why Preston offered a stapler rather than push-pins. Believe it or not, people are so trifling, they'll steal the push-pins off the board and leave the papers on the ground, and guess who's going have to clean up after them? Me and Preston.

It doesn't matter to Principal Vickins that some random student had left the flyers all over the floor. We're the ones hanging them up, so we're the ones that have to clean them up.

I looked at Nathan as he eyed at the remaining stack of flyers I had yet to hang up on the boards. I was nowhere near finished. His eyes were wide. "Dexter's working you guys ragged, huh?" He then reached down and took a flyer. "Seems like a lot for one person, you know?" A faint chuckle slipped from his lips and I felt my body stiffen.

It wasn't that I didn't want him around. It was just a little weird that he was even talking to me. Usually Nathan never talks to me. I mean, yeah, we knew each other last year because we had a class together, but that didn't mean we spoke to each other. (We were both in the same music class together. Surprisingly, Nathan was a natural in that class. I'm surprised Mr. Kioshi wasn't trying to recruit him to join the school's choir. Then again, Nathan was with

Diana at the time, so, I doubt Nathan would've even considered.)

Nathan had a smug look on his face when he offered to staple one of the flyers, and I sighed. He had good intentions but I didn't need him to just take over. I was perfectly fine without him.

I mean, I don't know. I could've used the extra help, I thought, but I was never sure about anything when it came to Nathan. He was like a Rubik's cube. Some people can figure him out on the first try, but not me. Even when he's trying to be transparent, he's complicated. What was his angle?

"Don't you have other places to be or something?" I blurted, immediately regretting the words that escaped from my mouth. The look on his face made a giant ball form in my throat. I lowered my gaze. "I didn't mean it like that, I was just curious is all."

"It's okay," I heard him say. Lies.

I reached for another flyer and positioned it on the corner of the bulletin board. Nathan grabbed my hand before I even had the chance to press the stapler against the paper.

"Mind if I give it a go?" he offered, keeping his voice straight. "It's just every time you do it, the stapler gets stuck." He pressed his lips together in a nervous smile, wrinkling his eyebrows.

I took a step to the side and handed Nathan the stapler. He adjusted the flyer on the board so it was straight. He pressed the stapler into the board and let out a sharp breath when he pulled back a little, detaching the stapler from the board with no problem.

He whipped his head around and his eyes lowered to the stack of flyers by my feet. "Another?"

My lips parted and I wanted to tell him that he didn't have to do anything else, but he reached down and took a flyer from the pile and stapled it to the other corner of the board.

He had this look about him that made him seem a bit more pleasing than how he used to be. It was as if he was finally able to let his true colors show without a wave of anxiety hammering down on him. I told myself that maybe Christopher was right. Maybe Nathan was just trying to be decent.

Though, it still stuns me that he was once friends with Christopher and Donny. It's hard to picture them all laughing together, especially since Donny can hardly stand Nathan's presence. He's made that pretty clear on multiple occasions. And yet, once upon a time, they could be civil to each other. Donny would laugh with him, and Nathan would probably talk to Donny the same way Christopher talks to him.

I wonder what happened between them?

Donny says that *"Diana happened"*, but that could mean anything. Maybe Diana changed Nathan in the worst way imaginable? Maybe she convinced him to leave Donny and Christopher behind and treat them as though they were nothing?

But who am I to ask? It's something Donny clearly doesn't like talking about, and I sure as hell am not asking Christopher or Nathan. They'll probably hate talking about it just as much as Donny would have.

Anyway, as I watched Nathan staple his fifth flyer to a different billboard, I cleared my throat and thanked him for offering to help. I could've done the rest on my own, but he just kept telling me that he didn't mind. He was like, "It's no problem, I got it. I have nothing better to do anyway."

I snorted. "That's a first." I meant to keep that to myself.

Nathan pressed his lips together in a flat line and drifted his gaze downward. I felt a strange knot form in my stomach when I saw the look on his face. "I didn't mean it like that, I was just—"

"—surprised I would even talk to you?" He didn't sound frustrated or upset with me. In fact, he was smirking as he spoke to me. He took a step forward towards me and sighed. "You wouldn't be the first person to think that way about me, I guess. I can't say I don't deserve it because I do. But that guy who messed with you earlier in the year, that's not me. I don't even know why I even did that, you know?" He leaned against the wall, his eyes now looking down at his fingers.

It took a lot of guts for him to even say something like that, to be honest. I could tell he was really trying to do better—which proved Christopher right. Nathan was just trying to be decent. He's still trying. He was comfortable enough to talk to me without fearing whatever I had to say. He was finally starting to get his head out of the gutter.

Breaking up with that bimbo Diana Clovis was probably the best thing for him. He won't admit it, but I can see it.

I saw it in his eyes. He didn't look so drained. He actually seemed alive, like his soul was no longer trapped in some box. He could say whatever was on his mind, do whatever he truly desired.

He seemed better—I think. He sure sounded better.

The bell sounded, signaling the end of fourth period. Before Nathan could walk away, I reached for his arm and he turned around to face me. I felt my body stiffen and I tried to find the right words to say. I could've just let him go without even saying anything at all. I just couldn't.

I let go of his arm and folded my arms over my chest. "I forgive you," I said, my voice practically shaking. "Like we're good."

Nathan's eyebrows lifted and his lips parted. "Really?"

I shrugged. "Yeah." I hardly sounded convincing.

He opened his mouth, ready to say something else, but then he froze. He was looking over my shoulder and when I looked behind me, I saw Diana walking up the hallway with Austin Brown's arm around her. She wasn't smiling but she didn't seem miserable either. Austin was rambling and she just listened to him as they continued to walk up the hallway. I looked back at Nathan. His jaw tightened and his nostrils flared.

"Nathan?" I rested my hand on his shoulder and he shook his head, taking a step back.

"I'm good," he huffed, his eyes avoiding me. "I'll catch you later, Meagan." Then he was gone.

After that, I didn't see Nathan for the rest of the day. I had gathered the rest of the flyers and I heard Preston call out my name from behind me. I noticed that he had a couple of flyers left over, but not as many as I had. His eyes nearly popped out of his head when he saw that I still had a big stack of flyers left.

"Did you even try?" he asked, snorting. He reached and took half of the stack off of my hands. "How many did you even get up? Two?"

I rolled my eyes. "It's my fault," I told him. "Nathan even

helped but the stupid stapler would get stuck sometimes."

Preston arched an eyebrow. "Nathan? Hendricks?" He started looking around at the different students walking past us, and then shifted his attention back to me. "You're telling me that Nathan Hendricks helped you put up these flyers?"

I rolled my eyes. "Look, I'm not kidding with you, okay? He did. I was struggling getting these things up, so."

Preston let out a sharp sigh and pursed his lips. He nodded his head and said, "If that's the case, more flyers should've been up", and then he turned on his heels and left. I really couldn't stand Preston at times—and this was one of those times.

The rest of the day was uneventful and my plans to tell my friends about my upcoming surgery was a total no-go. I had thought about maybe sending them a text message about it, but it wouldn't have been right. I wasn't chickening out, it's just—I thought I owed it to them to be up-front with them about the whole thing in-person rather than behind a screen. It's bad enough that I told them about my heart condition through a text message.

I don't want to be known as that person who seems too afraid to discuss things face-to-face. It's sort of cowardly. But I'll figure things out. I usually do.

Your Friend,

Meagan Wright

SENT: December 19th, 2012

Lee,

Things went better than I expected when I told my friends about my surgery. I found the opportunity to tell them during lunch, but it was a bit of a spontaneous move. I didn't strategize a way to bring it up, it just slipped out—and it really caught them all of guard. But they were chill about it which put me at ease.

Christopher even patted me on the back and told me, "You got a lot of heart, love." I found myself smiling like a dork and he ruffled my hair. I wasn't even upset about it.

The only thing that would've made things better was if Moe and Donny had been there too. Neither of them were in school today. Quite frankly, they spend more days out of school than actually in school. It's surprising how they manage to keep their grades up since they're hardly in school.

But it's not like they don't have a reason for their absences. Last time they were out of school, their grandmother had died. So maybe something else happened and they had to stay home. I didn't want to poke my nose where it shouldn't have been, but I still wanted to let them know about my surgery.

So, I asked Christopher if he thought it would've been a good idea for me to visit Donny and Moe after school, and tell them about my surgery. He shrugged his shoulders, insisting that it wouldn't be a terrible thing to do.

"You told us, why not tell 'em?"

I shrugged. "Usually when they're out of school, something is up. I didn't know if it would've been a bad call."

Christopher gulped down the chocolate milk that was already in his mouth, and he smacked his lips. "They probably just slept in. I talked to Don earlier, he seemed fine."

I thought it was pretty weird for Donny and Moe to miss out on a whole day of school just to sleep-in, but Christopher knew Donny like the back of his hand. So I took his word for it.

After school, I caught the train and took the bus straight to Donny and Moe's place. I sent my mom a text message as I got off the bus, letting her know that I had to swing over to Donny's place for a bit to get some notes for our class. (Technically, there was some truth in what I was saying.) I didn't want her to worry about me or freak out about me not coming home straight from school.

I felt my heart pounding rapidly the farther I walked down the block to get to Donny's place. I put one of my earbuds in my ears to listen to some music, hoping that would calm my nerves. I knew it was all in my head and that I was just nervous. Yet, as I continued to walk down to their house, something in my gut was telling me that things weren't okay. Something was wrong.

I kept telling myself to stop overthinking, but the knots in my stomach kept getting worse and worse. I had to take a couple deep breaths before I even had the guts to head up to the front door of their house. *Get your head out of the gutter*, I told myself.

When I came up to the house, I noticed that the garage door was open and I could see Donny moving around inside. When I took a closer look, everything was different. The garage was completely emptied out. The sofa and the leather reclining chairs were gone, the rug was rolled up against the door with the cooler underneath, the table was pushed to the back of corner of the garage, the record player was nowhere in sight, and all the CDs and books and vinyl records that were once on the shelves were now packed up in boxes. The only things that stayed the same were the little decorative lights on the walls. It looked like a regular garage with storage pushed off to the side in boxes.

Donny's car was parked inside the garage and he was on his knees, unscrewing one of the tires. He was so focused on his car that he didn't see me walk up to him. It wasn't until he was finished unscrewing the tire from the car that he looked up and realized that I was standing over him.

"Hey," he huffed, locking his eyes on me.

"Hey," I said, scratching my eyebrow. "How are you?"

Donny shrugged his shoulders, wiping his hands with the cloth that he left over his shoulder. "Not too bad." When he finally stood up, I noticed the dark circles under his eyes. By the looks of it, I doubt he even slept in like Christopher had assumed. "What's up with you?" He settled his hands on his hips, a faint smirk curling on his lips.

"Not much, I guess."

Even though we were sort of the same height, I actually felt shorter than him. It wasn't that I was scared of him, I just didn't know what to think of him at the time. He made me question whether or not it was a good idea for me to even be there. He didn't say anything but he sort of looked down at me a bit and I hardly had the audacity to look him in the eyes.

Finally, I cleared my throat and asked him if he was busy, which was pretty dumb since I was obviously interrupting him from working on his car. I figured he'd probably tell me that he was, but instead, he snickered, saying he had all the time in the world. I thought he was being sarcastic, but he gestured for me to follow him outside and we sat on the curb.

Donny pulled his knees in close to his chest and twisted the cloth in his hands. My lips were suddenly dry but I didn't have any chap-stick on me, not that I even bothered checking anyway.

"What's on your mind?" he suddenly asked.

I thought of what to say. I knew what I wanted to say, but I just wanted to make sure I said everything just right, you know? I didn't want to give him a scare and make him think that the reason why I needed surgery was because something was wrong with me. Nothing was wrong with me. I just needed a battery replacement for my defibrillator. That's all I told him too.

I let him know that I would be out of school for a bit at the start of the new semester due to my surgery. I explained to him that it was only for a battery replacement for my defibrillator, and I told him that I would be fine. I knew I was going to be fine. I've had plenty of heart surgeries before—this was just a battery.

Nothing too bad.

Donny's eyes were locked on me the whole time and he tightly pressed his lips together in a thin line. My skin felt warm when he gently bumped his fist against my arm and muttered something in Spanish at first.

"You're tough, kid. Don't worry about it," he added through soft chuckles.

It felt as though I could breathe again.

"You don't have to call me that all the time you know."

"Do you want me to stop?" he asked, arching his eyebrow.

I shook my head, a soft chuckle escaping my lips. "Nah, it's cool. I just think it's funny sometimes, you calling me that. I'm not *that* much younger than you."

Donny snorted. "Well, to be fair, it is your fault." When I arched my eyebrows, his cheeky grin started to form. "You called me *'Donny'*, so I get to call you *'kid'*, remember?"

He was right. Even though I didn't necessarily tell him that he had to call me *"kid"*, when I called him *"Donny"*, it sort of gave him the go-ahead, I guess. It's just our thing.

We started talking about random things, like school and how much we were ready for it to be over. Donny was set on graduating and was already sending in applications for college. He didn't tell me where he was planning on going exactly, but I figured he'd go to whatever school offered him the most money.

He said that he thought about skipping out on college for a while, or if he had to, he'd go to community college and just work part-time somewhere. But Moe didn't want that for him. He said that she wanted him to apply somewhere far to get the hell away from this place—away from home and out of Philly.

"She'd beat the shit out of me if I stayed. She told me herself." He was shaking his head, looking down at the ground. "If only I could take her with me. Maybe it'd be easier for the both of us."

That sounded pretty funny coming from the guy who thought it'd be a good idea to send her to some rehabilitation center in Texas. I know it's not the same and that sending her somewhere that would help her was a good thing, but she's still going to be away from everyone. Away from her parents and Donny, away from us—her friends. It's not fair, and I know for a fact, that's not something she wants.

I thought about how much this was probably killing her. I know Donny has the best intentions and wants the best for her, but he doesn't know what's best for her because he's not her. It sounds corny but it's true. I thought back to what she told me on the day of Carmen's little cousin's birthday party—she wants a brother, not a caretaker. He of all people should at least understand how much this is going to kill her, right? I don't even know why he would think it was a good idea.

So I asked him, "Do you really think sending her to Texas will help, then? She'll be far from everyone she cares about."

Donny bit the inside of his cheek and started tapping his foot. I thought lasers were going to shoot from his eyes by the way he was glaring at me. I looked away from him, already regretting that I said anything. But it probably had to be said. I mean, he probably didn't even think of how far she'd be from everyone. Even if he did, it was crazy to send her away to Texas on her own.

Still, I could've brought it up better. I didn't have to call him out the way I did. I mean, I didn't mean to make him look like the bad guy.

I let out a sharp breath. "Donny I didn't mean to—"

"—to make it sound like you know this shit better than I do?" He was trying not to yell, even though he was on the brink of yelling. His voice would get a little quiet but then he'd speak up again so I could hear him. When I finally had the courage to look him in his eyes, I saw nothing but flames. Yet, he didn't raise his voice at me once. His nostrils flared and he shifted his eyes forward to look out towards the street. "I appreciate the efforts, kid, but this is something that doesn't require much of your opinion. It's something we have to deal with as a family, and it's totally different from what you already think of it."

The way Donny said *"kid"* this time felt like a punch to the gut. I figured I was probably crossing the line by say something in the first place, but hearing the way he called me *"kid"* was his way of telling me, *screw off.* His eyebrows wrinkled from bitter irritation and he started mumbling in Spanish, still looking away from me.

I opened my mouth to tell him something—perhaps *"I'm sorry"* if it'd help—but Donny stood up off the ground and dusted the back of his pants. He settled his hands on his hips, keeping his jaw tight. When he looked at me, every bodily function had shut down. His gaze pierced into my soul like daggers and I suddenly forgot how to breathe.

Donny wiped his hands with the small cloth in his hands, and then he threw the cloth over his shoulder. He sighed deeply while rubbing his head with his hand.

"It's getting kind of late and I know how your mom gets." He spoke softly as he stood over me as if he were a giant. "I'd drive you home but the car, ya know? Still working on it."

"Oh," I muttered. "Right." I stood up.

I knew he was trying to get rid of me. I honestly didn't blame him. Although, he was getting rid of me at a decent time. I had to get home before the street lights turned on or else mom would've killed me. She'd bombard me with so many questions, asking what had taken me so long to come home, insisting that I should've called her and asked her to pick me up or something. I didn't want to deal with that when I got home.

Luckily, I didn't have to because she wasn't even home yet.

I let out a sigh of relief, thanking God. Yet, I still couldn't get Donny out of my mind. I couldn't forget his face or the sound of his voice. He probably wanted to cuss me out, tell me to get over myself for thinking I knew better than he did when it came to Moe. That was a lie, I didn't think I knew better than him. I just wanted him to think things over a bit more, you know?

He wasn't trying to be selfish, but just forcing Moe to go somewhere without having her input—it wasn't right. He still insists that the situation was different from what I already thought of it, but I don't see it that way. The both of us probably were probably in the wrong here.

Your Friend,

Meagan Wright

SENT: December 21st, 2012

Lee,

The past few days have been brutal with the approach of winter break. Mr. Rover gave us back our essays on our assigned book reflections. Not to brag but I'm pretty proud of myself

When Mr. Rover handed me my essay, I could tell from the look on his face that I deserved the grade he gave me.

An A-plus.

Although, I was a little shocked. I'm not going to say that I didn't bullshit some parts of my essay, because I did, which is why I'm surprised he didn't give me a lower grade. I wasn't going to complain about it though. I was probably one of the three students who earned an A-plus on their papers. It was a relief.

Still, he assigned us work to do over the break. He wanted us to complete our grammar packets in addition to writing a five-page paper, single-spaced, on the significant message the authors were trying to convey from the books we've read.

The class groaned.

Five pages and single-spaced—why not just shoot us?

I don't know what different books he assigned for everyone else to read, but he assigned me to read a Jace Gregg book. There's only so much I can learn from Jace Gregg.

He's an author of fictional romance and unlikely outcomes.

It's great content, not going to lie, but how can something like that be significant? It's not like I can relate to the characters easily. Unlike me, the characters always manage to get their lives together.

Something I'm still struggling to do.

That's why I enjoy reading his books—to get a break from my own life. I can't say the same for other people who read his books, like Benton for example.

Benton started reading *A Thing So Magnificent*, which was Jace Gregg's recently released book, and Benton is in-love with it. He thinks the characters are absolutely real, and the story offered him all the answers on how to navigate his life without fail.

"I've never related so much to people who don't even exist."

I'll be honest, I felt like that for a while after reading *The Infinite Dynamic of Claud & Francis* for the first time, but then I had to learn that fiction was fiction for a reason. Some people crave the life of fiction, where things usually work out. Sometimes it does, sometimes it doesn't.

But if everything always worked out, the story would be boring as hell. At least that's how I see it.

Anyway, Christopher had asked us if we could help him clean out his garage after school since his dad was planning on setting up a garage sale this weekend. So, Peter, Carmen, Benton, and I went over to Christopher's place to help him out with going through the storage in the garage.

Their garage was huge—big enough to fit three cars. And yet, instead of fitting three cars, it was filled with boxes containing knick-knacks, antiques, dusty oil paintings, and fine china plates.

(Half the stuff we found I wanted to take home and keep for myself, but I wouldn't know where to put them in my house. Mom would probably sit them in the corner somewhere and let them get all dusty.)

I was going through my second box of storage when Christopher asked me about my conversation with Donny the other day. The question came out of his mouth effortlessly.

I sighed. "Could've been better, I guess," was all I could say.

I honestly didn't want to think about it. I could still remember Donny's face when I questioned him about sending Moe away to Texas. In that moment, I honestly thought he hated me. I could've kept my mouth shut and I probably should've, but I wouldn't be able to live with myself if I hadn't said anything.

I couldn't be a coward, I wouldn't be able to even look at myself in the mirror. But if I had known he'd be that pissed off from me saying anything, I would've chosen my words very carefully. Maybe the conversation would've ended better.

Christopher suddenly crouched down so he met my eye-level. I tried to focus on going through the box, but Christopher's eyes remained on me as if he was trying to crack open my skull with his mind. I looked up at him and forced a smile on my face just to get him off my back. When I uttered the words, "I'm fine, Chris", and he snorted, rolling his eyes.

I furrowed my eyebrows. "What? I am."

"You don't seem fine to me." He rocked forward so he was leaning in close to me. "I thought you just told him about your surgery? How'd that go wrong?"

I finally sat down on the ground and a chill shot through my body. I pulled my knees in close to my chest and buried my face in my arms. Christopher had a point. Looking back, if I had just told Donny about my surgery, I wouldn't have pissed him off.

When I explained to Christopher everything that actually happened—that I questioned Donny sending Moe away to Texas—he just stared at me. His lips were parted and he remained silent. He probably agreed with me, thinking the whole thing was a ridiculous idea and that it wasn't the best decision, but he didn't say anything. He just settled himself down beside me and pulled his knees in close to his chest, letting out a sigh. His arms came around my shoulder and I shivered at the touch.

"You cold?" he asked, looking at me.

"A little." My voice quivered. "But it's alright."

Christopher took off his jacket and threw it on around me. I felt my body suddenly relax as my head rested against his shoulder. He threw his head back against the wall, groaning and rubbing his eyes.

"It's not your fault, love," he said through his thick Irish accent. "I get it. You try to talk to him but it feels as though you're getting nowhere. I tried that a couple times. At the end of the day, tell you the truth, we don't even know what's best for ourselves. So who are we to say anything at times?"

I then realized that he had a point. We don't even know what's best for ourselves. It's infuriating because it's like an endless game of cat-and-mouse— chasing after a solution to figure out our own shit, but nothing seems to work and we're right back where we started.

I lifted my head off of Christopher's shoulder and I looked at him as his lashes fluttered shut. His nostril sort of flared. I could tell he was over everything. I could tell by the way his jaw tightened, he didn't want to talk or think about Donny. There was nothing I could say to really lighten the mood, but even if I had, I'm sure it wouldn't have done much.

Christopher then patted my knee and stood up with his lips pressed together in a flat line. He stretched his arms until a loud crack sound was heard, coming from his bones. (My mom hates it when I crack my bones, but it's always so satisfying.)

I handed Christopher back his jacket and thanked him for allowing me to borrow it. Without warning, Christopher's arms were around me, pulling me into his warm, lean body. He was actually stronger than I would've expected. It's no wonder he always managed to take Peter down in a swift move.

And I felt so short and little in his arms. He was a bit taller, but he wasn't much of a giant either compared to other guys. Still, he definitely wasn't short. I eventually melted into the hug and didn't want him to let me go, but that would've been too much. (God forbid Carmen saw us and got the wrong idea.)

I noticed Peter standing behind us with his arms crossed over his chest and a mischievous smirk curling on his lips. I gave Christopher a quick pat on the back and wiggled out of the hug. I looked at Christopher in the eyes, His eyes were getting glossy but he blinked so tears wouldn't fall.

I didn't think he was going to cry. At least, I didn't think so at the time. I couldn't imagine Christopher crying. I mean, I'm pretty sure he'd cry over great tragedies, but not over BS. If anything, he'd be more annoyed over something like this. Nothing to cry over.

As he went off to go through more boxes, he hardly said a word to anyone. Peter nudged me as I polished one of the vases and he asked me if I knew what was going on with Christopher.

I shook my head, playing dumb. I only did it for Peter's sake. If I opened my mouth and told Peter what was going on, it would've destroyed him. Plus, Christopher and I were the only ones who knew about Moe being sent away to Texas, and quite frankly, we wanted to keep that way until Donny had the balls to actually bring it up to everyone else.

Peter sharply sighed. "I saw you two hugging, so what gives?"

I gulped, thinking of what to say. I had to be smart. "I've been having a rough day, thinking about the surgery and all. He was just giving me some encouragement."

Peter's face softened and his lips sort of quivered. His arm draped over my shoulder and he rested his head against mine. "We're here for you, okay? Don't worry. You got this." He patted me on the back and went off to go through another storage box.

I started feeling a bit queasy as I watched Peter leave, and I leaned against the box. It was sick the way I lied to him like it was nothing. I wanted to kick myself all the way up to Mars.

I was honestly happy when we were finished going through everything because I was ready to go home and forget about today. I knew that I would face the wrath of my mom for getting home late, but it was better than thinking about Donny. It's not that I don't like thinking about him, I do. It's just that I hate the way things went down the other day. Then to see Christopher all upset about it only made things worse. I had to go home.

Benton and I were going to catch the bus home but Christopher offered us a ride. Peter and Carmen were probably going to spend the night over his place since Christopher told them that they could stay in the guest rooms.

Riding with Christopher felt different from when I would ride with Donny. It wasn't bad but it didn't feel good either. I think it was because I was so used to Donny having the radio blasting in his car. The silence in Christopher's car was so strange to me. I tried not to think about it and I just slipped on my earbuds and listened to some music during the ride.

When Christopher pulled up to my house, Benton hopped out the car and wished us a goodnight. I watched as he quickly walked across the street to get to his house. If my mom was going to be furious with me for being out so late, I'm sure Robyn was going to lay him out too. Even if he did call her and let her know where he was, it was still late and the street lights were on.

As I unbuckled to get out the car, Christopher reached for my hand and he huffed. His eyes remained locked on me as he told me to not worry myself to death over the things going on with Donny and Moe.

"It's out of your control with them, love. Believe it or not, he'll never say it aloud but he does love you. A lot." He chuckled scratching his eyebrow. "Probably bumped me to the bottom of his list, actually."

I snorted. I knew what type of love he was talking about—the platonic kind of love. I wouldn't have expected anything else, to be honest. I wanted to believe that Donny had some love for me, but at this point, he'll probably hardly tolerate me.

Even so, I know I love him. It may not be romantic but it's real. It's something I can't get over, and I didn't realize it until now. I wish I could go back to the other day, and tell Donny how I felt. I wish I could just throw my arms around him and tell him that even though I didn't agree with him on things, I still loved him. And I'd mean every word too.

I know if Christopher had the chance, he'd do the same exact thing. That's probably why he said what he had said before I got out of the car. But things weren't that easy, they're never that easy. But I guess the thought of things being that way will help me sleep better at night.

Your Friend,

Meagan Wright

SENT: December 26th, 2012

Lee,

Wishing someone a Merry belated-Christmas isn't a thing, but how else am I supposed to start off this email? I wasn't allowed on my computer at all yesterday because my mom wouldn't allow it, so today I'm wishing you a Merry belated-Christmas.

My mom and I didn't really do much for Christmas this year. We actually spent the entire day at home, just chilling. We called all the relatives to wish them a Merry Christmas, and I was on the phone with my dad for like an hour, catching up on things. He said he was going to swing by the house to see me on New Year's and I thought that was fine, but he still wanted my mom's approval to make sure it was okay.

"I just want to make sure, okay? Then get back to me on whatever she says," he said. He sounded hopeful, but he didn't want to give himself too much hope.

But my mom said it was fine. She talked to him herself. They were civil and she even laughed a little. I could hear him laughing on the other line too since my dad has such a loud laugh.

It wasn't weird that they were acting that way towards each other. I knew there was still much love between them, it was obvious. Some nights before bed, I'd think about things going back to the way they used to be—the three of us in one house, making memories and having a good laugh. But I don't know a thing about the way love works, it's a weird thing. They probably love each other the same way I love Donny—not romantically, but it's something real.

It's too much to think about, though.

A little later, mom and I decided to open our gifts. Mom got me a box-set of mismatched graphic socks, which I really did appreciate since socks were my way of creative expression through fashion. I could see the satisfied grin on my mom's face as I reached forward and wrapped my arms around her, thanking her for my gift. She pressed her lips to my forehead, telling me that she loved me.

It was then my turn.

I got her a pair of earrings and a nice diamond necklace that I saw in the window of a store downtown when I was hanging out with Benton not that long ago. (It was after school, I think.) I knew she would love it. She was the first person I thought of when I spotted the jewelry.

Her jaw nearly dropped to the floor when she opened the box and admired the earrings and necklace. I thought she was going to cry, so I wrapped my arms around her rubbed her back. She sucked her teeth, smiling at me. Then out of nowhere, she started bugging me about how much I spent on the jewelry. I just couldn't win.

"It was on sale, mom."

"Meagan...*how much?*"

"Fifty."

"That *includes* the earrings?"

"Yeees mom."

It was actually about a hundred-something dollars altogether, but it was for my mom. Call me daughter of the year.

As we were cleaning up the wrapping paper, my phone buzzed and I read the notification. It was a text message from Moe, asking me how I was doing. My heart quickened its pace. My mom asked me if everything was alright. I nodded my head, telling her that I was fine.

I started contemplating on how to respond to Moe's message. I knew I was overthinking and making a big deal out of nothing. I had to get a grip.

I responded to her message, telling her that I was fine, and then I asked her how things were for her. I thought about Donny before I hit SEND. I could've easily asked her how he's been as well, but maybe that would've made me seem clingy.

I was in my room, working on my assignments for school when I got a text message from Moe, telling me that she was going to call me tomorrow (which is today) so we could talk. I felt my heart dislodge from my chest and fall into the pit of my stomach.

What would she even want to talk about? Was it about Donny? Did she know about our conversation the other day?

Moe might not have been there but she lives with him, she's not stupid or blind. She knows when something is up.

I tried not to assume the worse. Even when I was on the phone with her today, I tried to keep things light and not let my nerves get to me. She called around noon-ish and mom had work, so I had the house to myself. When I answered the phone, I took a deep breath and spoke softly so that way I was able to remain calm.

"Hey, Moe. What's up?"

She answered, "Hey, Meagan."

At first, I didn't even know if it was her. She didn't sound like the Morris-Lina I had known. The girl on the phone sounded drained of life, as if she was struggling to keep herself together.

"You good?" I asked, my words sort of shaky.

"Yeah, why wouldn't I be?" She didn't sound too sure of herself, but she just gave me the easy answer so I wouldn't pry.

I cleared my throat and nodded. As she continued to talk, I was telling myself that everything was fine. I wanted to believe that she was going to be fine. If anything was wrong, she would've told me, but she didn't say anything. Instead, she asked me if I enjoyed the holiday, and I told her that everything was fine since my mom and I just lounged around.

Moe snickered on the other line. "I'm surprised you didn't spaz out. You weren't all drugged up were you?"

I rolled my eyes. "Give me a little more credit than that."

She scoffed, muttering something in Spanish before telling me, "Where's the fun in that?" She was starting to sound like her usual self again. I could hear it in the way she laughed and spoke.

The more we talked, I pictured that familiar dimpled smile she'd always have on her face. I thought about the way her eyes would light up every time a crazy thought came into her head, and how eager she'd be to spill it out. During most of the conversation, that's all I could think about—Moe acting and sounding like herself. Even if the thought didn't last long, it just felt good to even have it come to mind.

The idea of everything actually being okay.

We must've been on the phone for like two hours, talking about a bunch of nonsense. We didn't mention school or ask about each other's families. We just focused on each other, and to be honest, it felt great.

But it didn't last long, of course.

At some point, Donny was brought up in the conversation and it took everything in me to not sound like a total putz while on the phone. I cleared my throat about a dozen times and took a couple of deep breaths as she told me about him wanting her to go to a rehabilitation center in Texas in order to receive *"the best proper care"*.

She had scoffed, saying it was just a complete waste of time and money, but she knew she didn't have much of a say. She said, "If it'll get them to sleep at night, then what choice do I have? If you ask me, I bet they had this on their bucket list for a while."

The whole time, I just listened to her and kept my mouth shut.

She didn't know that I knew about her going away. She didn't even know about the little chat I had with Donny the other day either. Good, I wanted to keep it that way. But I thought it was pretty strange that she decided to talk about it, considering that she didn't know that I knew about it.

Did she trust me to not say anything to the others? Was that it?

I don't know. I didn't ask.

Instead, I pressed the phone to my ear and settled into my bed, pressing my back against my pillows. "I doubt that's something that'll be on someone's bucket list, Moe." I tried making a joke, but it wasn't funny.

Moe snorted. "I don't know. Maybe for my parents, but Donald has other plans I want him to focus on. Like what he's gonna do for college. He already has his eyes set on this school in Europe."

My body froze. I was so stiff I thought I was under paralysis, I couldn't move. My lips quivering and all I could control were my eyes. I could hear Moe saying my name on the other line but I couldn't open my mouth. All I kept thinking about were the words she had just said to me—about Donny going to Europe for college.

Donny. In Europe. For college.

It was on repeat in my head like a broken record player until I had finally snapped out of it. Moe was still on the phone and she said my name about a dozen more times. When I cleared my throat and told her that I was still on the phone, she let out a sigh.

"He didn't tell you about that one, did he?" There was a hint of guilt in her voice.

"No," I confessed, the words sounding as if I had been strangled due to the sudden dryness in my throat. I cleared my throat again. "We talked about him going to college. Like, he said he was applying, but he didn't say where."

I figured that the reason why Donny didn't say anything about it was probably because he thought it would've been too early for him to tell me anyways. I mean, he graduates in June, so he probably wanted to wait until like April or May to finally say something. Or maybe wait until he received a letter from the school, stating whether or not he was accepted.

I doubt he'd worry about that though. He could probably get

into whatever school was on his radar.

Him and Moe, but Moe wasn't planning on going to college. She told me that she wasn't like Donny and didn't have the motivation to even try. Even if she had the motivation, she thought it still wouldn't have worked out for her.

"I don't have dreams like Donald," she said in a clear voice. "He wants to specialize in medicine and do all these big things for other people. He never talks about things like that much, but when we were kids, that's all he's wanted to do. It's kind of weird when you think about it. No one on the block ever goes around, talking about *Donald Gonzalez, the boy with the brains*."

She started chuckling but I could tell it wasn't from amusement. I felt the knots in my stomach start to twist and I rolled over on my side. I tried telling her that she had just as much potential as he did, but she scoffed, insisting that I was lying to myself. I don't even know why she'd even think of something so ridiculous. She was still set on the idea, though. She thought Donny was better off in Europe, getting away from everything and everyone. She said that she had already convinced him to apply to two different schools in Europe that offered the best medical programs.

Welmur's University and Charleston Clinton University.

I've heard of both universities. (I think Welmur's is in Wales, and Charleston is in Scotland.)

Moe didn't give him much of a choice, she said. I could hear her words starting to break the more she talked about her wanting the best for him. She figured him leaving was the best for him. She didn't want to be the one holding him back.

But he's never thought of her holding him back. Never ever.

I wanted her to realize that she was doing everything right. Even when she thought things felt wrong, she was perfectly fine.

Before we ended the call, I told her that she was a good sister, and that Donny loved her more than she could imagine. Moe took what I said and rolled with it. She let out a sigh, telling me, "I know", and told me that she would talk to me later. I opened my mouth, wanting to tell her that I wished her the best, but she ended the call before I could even get a word out.

Usually I try not to dwell on things that are beyond my control. It's not an easy thing to do since I normally stress over little things. But it's like Christopher said, I couldn't stress over things like this. Although this wasn't what he was referring to, his claim still stands.

I couldn't stress over the fact that Donny was possibly going to be in another country after graduation and maybe never come back. I couldn't beat myself over the fact that Moe wouldn't acknowledge how great of a person she was for herself.

Still, she was my friend and I loved her.

Hearing her voice for the first time in a while was probably the highlight of my day. Maybe the highlight of my week.

Your Friend,

Meagan Wright

Lee,

I spent the day over grandma Gladys's house, but mom sort of made me go over. Her thing was: *"You spend too much time in this house, I need you to get out and do something. You seem miserable."*

Meanwhile, this is the same woman who flips out if I decide to take a stroll around the block, whether it be to the corner store or just for the heck of it. There's no winning with my mom. If I stay-in, she thinks I'm being depressed. If I go out, she worries herself almost to death.

(I think it's an inherited trait because grandma Gladys is the same way when it comes to mom. She'll get all worked up if mom doesn't answer the phone after two tries, and then she'll be so quick to get my mom out the house if she's feeling tired.)

Anyway, being over grandma Gladys's was pretty much a ticket to lazy town since there's never anything to do over there. I don't know what my mom was expecting when she came to pick me up and asked about my day. All I did was watch a few movies from the '60s with my grandmother, and then I took a terribly long nap since I left my books at home.

I was in the car, telling my mom about my day and she just shook her head. It took me a second to notice the faint smile curling on her face as she kept her eyes forward on the road. When she came to a red light, she glanced at me, pursing her lips.

"You should've brought a book."

I just looked at her. I knew better than to open my mouth and say something because if I did, my lips would be on the floor. So, I was smart and kept my mouth shut. I was quiet the entire ride, and mom played the gospel station to make up for the silence.

When we finally got home, it was dark and mom was thinking of ordering pizza since she was too tired to make anything. I told her that I would cook us something but she shook her head. She probably wasn't in the mood for breakfast food since that's all I really knew how to make. So many times mom would try to show me how to make other dishes, but I never really paid any attention to what she was doing.

One time, mom tried to show me how to make pasta pie, which was something grandma Gladys used to make and was one of my mother's favorite dishes. But everything my mom tried to teach me went in one ear and out the other. I honestly felt like the worst daughter ever. It's now a rarity for mom to find the time to show me how to make anything, and that was the only time she tried to show me how to make something other than breakfast food.

So one day, I went over to grandma Gladys's house and she taught me how to make pasta pie. On that same night, I made it for mom when she came home from work. The way her eyes sparkled when she took a bite out of it, it made me feel complete.

Still, besides pasta pie, breakfast food is always my go-to. I once made my mom a French omelet and she was blown away. But she wasn't in the mood for that tonight. Besides, I don't even think we have enough eggs for me to make us omelets.

Anyway, my mom and I were getting out the car and we suddenly heard someone calling our names. We looked across the street and saw Robyn waving to us while sitting on her porch with Han, Roselle, and Benton. They looked like the perfect family, just chilling outside on a nice breezy day.

Honestly, they would've been a perfect portrait.

My mom waved back to Robyn, forcing a faint smile on her face to hide the tiredness in her eyes. I stayed behind my mom as she took a few steps forward into the street. Robyn came down from their porch and stood on the sidewalk

Their voices echoed throughout the neighborhood but no one would step outside to complain. It's normal for people to call out to each other in our neighborhood. Happens all the time like any other neighborhood.

I noticed Benton looking at me as I stood behind my mom as she and Robyn carried on with their loud conversation. He had his headphones shifted his focus back to his phone.

Robyn offered us leftovers she had from last night's dinner. I remember her going into the house for a second and coming back out with two paper plates wrapped up in aluminum foil. I was hardly paying attention to anything my mom and Robyn were saying, and I hardly noticed Robyn coming over from across the street to meet us with the plates of food.

"It's one of Han's favorite dishes." Robyn dropped the plates into my mom's arms. "His mother taught me a long time ago before she passed. We used to cook together all the time."

My mom smiled, her eyes becoming glossy. She was tired, and

this was probably overwhelming for her. All Robyn did was offer us some food and my mom thought she was a life savior. Mom was too tired to cook and probably too tired to wait for the delivery man if she had ordered us food.

Mom let out a sound that sort of startled me. I was certain she was going to start crying but she didn't shed a tear. She had a smile plastered on her face and she let out a sigh of relief.

Robyn sort of mimicked her smile and brought her hand to mom's shoulder. "If you don't like it, it's okay," Robyn said, still holding the smile on her face.

Mom shook her head, chuckling. "I know it's delicious. Don't be silly, Robyn. I just wish I could repay you."

"Don't. Your daughter being such a joy is enough."

Mom's eyes were on me now. She faintly smiled at me and I could tell that she was close to tears. I knew she was very tired. She gets emotional when she's exhausted. The last thing I wanted was for Robyn to think it was her fault if my mom suddenly busted into tears. Then Benton would come over and ask me if something was wrong, and I'd have to explain to him that everything was fine, even though things wouldn't have looked fine.

So I thanked Robyn for the food. I wished her a goodnight and told her that I would see them around. Well, "I'll see you later", is what I actually said.

I always see them because I always see Benton. Almost every day, actually.

Mom was quick to get in the house afterwards. She wasted no time hanging her jacket up in the closet and she plopped down on the couch. I snickered as she kicked off her heels and took the hair pins out of her hair, loosening her weave.

"Would you like me to draw you a bath, your highness?" I feigned a terrible British accent and my mom scowled at me.

Mom huffed as she rolled her eyes and waved her hand, basically shooing me away. I felt my phone vibrate in my pants pocket and I saw that Benton had sent me a text message. I read his text as I walked up the steps and made my way into my room.

- **Srry about my mom. She crazy too you know.**

I laughed as I plopped down on my bed. I sent him a laughing emoji and messaged him: **no worries, moms are always crazy lol.**

All of a sudden, a notification pops up on my phone that Moe had sent me a text message. I opened the message and I felt my chest tighten. The message started with her thanking me for our phone conversation the other night since she really missed me and was hesitant on calling me. She said she was hesitant to reach out to any of us after the incident at Kenny's Dine-n-Dash, but she finally decided to just send out individual text messages, asking us how we were doing.

I'm certain Christopher at least got back to her, and Peter as well. I know Carmen's been a little uneasy around Moe since the incident but she's still her friend.

And Benton.

Well, I don't know.

I just don't know how he feels about Moe. I know he tolerates her, but I don't know if he really looks at her as a friend. He'd just get real squeamish around her, as if he didn't know how to react when she said or did certain things. He would look away from her sometimes too. He'd laugh if she said something really funny, but that was a rarity—him laughing at her jokes.

(Moe's really out of pocket most of the time.)

Anyway, Moe's text message was like a friggin' novel but the more I read it, the more I was taken aback by her words. She said that even though we've only met just this year, she considered me as one of her great friends and thanked me for taking the time to talk to her the other day.

She told me that she wanted me to care of myself and to focus on my dreams. She thought Donny and I were the same since we both had big dreams to fulfill, and all she wanted was for us to do everything we could in order to make them come true.

Her text message almost had me in tears, and then I read the last few words to her message.

I love you just as much.

I love you just as much. Her literal words.

I must've read those words a few times more, and then I placed my phone down the dresser beside my bed. I was contemplating whether I should respond or let things be.

How would I even respond to something like that? Something so thought-provoking and deep? I was nearly in tears while reading the text message. That's how much it struck me. That's how much it mattered.

I eventually went downstairs to join my mom for dinner and I purposely left my phone upstairs, hoping that would help me figure out what to say in response to Moe's message. It didn't. After I finished eating and helped my mom clean the dishes, I went back upstairs to my room and I plopped down on my bed, just eyeing my phone.

I'm still looking back and forth between my phone and my computer, still hoping that something will come to me. No such luck. But knowing Moe, she probably wasn't really looking for a response anyway. This was probably just her way of saying *'thanks and no worries'*.

Your Friend,
Meagan Wright

Lee,

There is no better way to start this email off than wishing you a Happy New Year! It's a miracle from God that we made it this far in the game, can you believe it? All the doubters can go crawl under a rock with their crazy conspiracies on the world coming to an end.

Ha! We sure showed them, didn't we?

(My mom says "hi" by the way, just wanted to let you know. How are things in Australia with the start of a new year? I hope your family is doing well. Tell everyone we said "hi".)

This morning, I woke up to the sound of fireworks going off at six-something in the morning. I was annoyed—pissed off, actually. No one knew where the fireworks were coming from, but most of the neighbors had assumed it was some kids setting them off at the playground, but it was hard to tell. We just heard them going off and it was becoming annoying.

It's one thing to set fireworks off at midnight, it's another thing to set them off at six-something in the friggin' morning. Benton had sent me a text message a little after I was awakened from the ruckus, asking me if someone was shooting outside. I chuckled. It wasn't the idea of bullets flying everywhere that I thought was funny, it was the fact that he couldn't tell the difference between fireworks and bullets.

But then again, he hasn't lived here as long as I have, so he probably wasn't used to all the loudness.

I responded to his message with a laughing emoji and told him that it was fireworks, not bullets.

He replied: **I knew it! My mom doesn't listen :(**

I was still in bed when Benton sent me another text, asking when I had to check into the hospital for my surgery and I sighed. I didn't want to think about my surgery.

I mean, there's no avoiding it. It has to happen or else my heart is screwed. Again.

I was wishing that I didn't have a heart condition in the first place. I wouldn't have to miss the first week of school and I could see my friends, give them all a big hug to start off the new year. Everything would have felt normal, really normal. I would've felt normal. I didn't have to worry and wonder if people were just being nice to me because they felt sorry for me.

I know my friends don't feel that way, but some people do.

I guess it doesn't matter. People will always think what they want to think, and sometimes they're just hopeless—Donny told me that once. He ain't ever lie.

Anyway, I responded to Benton's message and told him that I had to check into the hospital this evening, but my mom and I were leaving this afternoon to beat traffic.

He sent me a heart emoji and told me to be safe.

I told him that I would be fine.

My mom eventually came into my room, demanding me to start getting dressed and to pack up whatever I needed to bring during my stay at the hospital. She made it clear that the bag wasn't big enough to carry everything in my room since I have a bad habit of overpacking. But I've gotten better over time. I'm now able to rule out what I will and will not use or wear. I know myself better. So she has to give me some credit for that at least.

It didn't take me long to get my stuff together this morning. I got up, got dressed, and packed up my things. I only really needed my school books, my laptop, undergarments, and a different outfit to wear for when I'm discharged from the hospital.

I didn't really take much. Well, to be honest, other than my school books, I didn't really need much. Even though I wouldn't be in school for the week, Principal Vickins assured me that she would choose a fellow student to be my informant so that way I wasn't behind on my assignment. (Informants are students chosen and trusted by the principal to keep absent students updated on their school assignments. The informants are responsible for giving absent students their assignments and returning the assignment to their student's teachers once they were completed.)

I'm honestly interested to know who Principal Vickins will choose to be my informant. Knowing her, she's probably going to choose someone I don't know.

Mom whipped us up a quick breakfast before we left—some eggs with buttered toast. We said a prayer before we dug in, and as we're eating, I felt mom staring at me the whole time. I looked up at her and she pressed her lips into a tight smile and her eyes became glossy.

I knew that look.

I reached across the table and grasped her hand into mine. Her long nails grazed against the back of my hand, but I didn't mind. I could feel mom's hand shaking a little as I held it in mine. She was nervous, no doubt, but I wanted her to know that everything would be okay.

I told her, "Love you, ma."

She let out a deep sigh and kissed the back of my hand.

"I know baby." She tried to mask her uncertainty with a smile.

After we finished eating and cleaned the kitchen, mom was in hustle mode. She made it clear that she didn't have the time nor the patience for lollygagging.

"We gotta beat traffic," she said, even though the chances of us getting stuck in traffic on a Saturday afternoon were slim to none.

It didn't take us long to get to the hospital, which wasn't surprising. Without traffic, it's only a fifteen minute drive, so we had enough time. But I guess in my mom's head, it didn't matter. She wanted us to get there as soon as possible. I don't know why she was in such a rush. Sure, it took a while for us to check-in since it's a hospital, but other than that, everything was fine.

As we sat in the waiting room, my phone started blowing up. My mom looked at me and was like, "Look at Miss Popular over here, blowing up." Only she finds her jokes funny, but for once I just went along with it.

I felt my heart pound heavily in my chest when I saw all the text messages from Carmen, Peter, Christopher, and Benton. Carmen's message was long and contained more emojis than actual words, but the emojis added emphasis to her kind words. There were a bunch of hearts and heart-eyed emojis, and she basically wished me luck on my surgery.

- **Missing you already! I'll keep you in my prayers! Love you lots!**

Peter's message didn't contain hundreds of emojis. He sent a GIF of a woman screaming, *"I love you!"*, in the pouring rain, and he sent a follow-up text, telling me that I was strong and that he believed in me.

- **My abuela always tells me God never gives us more than we can bear, I know you can bear this, you are so strong, GOD! You are like superhuman girl, damn! I love you!**

Christopher and Benton, on the other hand, kept their messages brief. They both wished me good luck with my surgery and said that they would be thinking of me. I honestly appreciated all of them. I messaged all them individually, thanking them for their love and support.

Once my name was finally called, mom sprung up from her seat and snatched up my bag. I could tell she was exhausted and probably didn't get much sleep last night—not surprised. Luckily, she was able to sit down in the guest chair once we arrived to my room as I was getting situated. I was placed in the Cardiac Care Unit and it was such a hassle being hooked up to the heart monitor, and then having to wait for my IV to be injected felt like an eternity.

Soon enough, one of the male nurses came in and offered to turn on the television as I waited for the nurses to do my IV. His name was Malakai and he looked a lot like Donny, only he was a bit older and had a few tattoos on his arms. He was cute.

I thanked him when he clicked on the television and placed the remote on the tray beside me.

"If you need anything just hit the buzzer, okay?"

I nodded and he left, closing the door behind him.

Mom chuckled under her breath, and I turned my attention over to her. She started wiggling her eyebrows and I almost gagged.

"He cute." She was so blunt, but she didn't care. "And he a Christian. I saw the Cross necklace on him. If only he was around your age, y'all would be perfect."

In the nick of time, the nurses came in, ready to put in my IV. I let out a sigh of relief. *Thank you, Father God.* (Proof that God hears and knows all.)

I tried keeping myself distracted by watching television as the nurses poked me a million times with the needle, trying to find a vein. The young nurse, a woman with strawberry blonde hair and big eyes like a cartoon character, kept apologizing and was close to tears when she saw how much I was in pain each time she jabbed me with the needle. The other nurse, a much older woman with hair like snow and eyes like crystals, told the younger nurse to keep herself together and to focus.

I let out another sharp breath and soon enough, it was finished. The strawberry blonde nurse apologized for the millionth time in the sweetest voice. I kind of felt bad for her. I could tell that the older nurse wasn't too pleased with how the younger nurse conducted things, but it was probably her first time doing something like this. Besides, the older nurse could've at least taken over and demonstrated how it's supposed to be done if things weren't going smoothly. But I'm not involved in nursing, so what do I know?

My arm still hurts when I move it, but I'm sure as the days go by, the pain will go away. Hopefully. Prayerfully. My God, it hurts. And I feel bad asking if the nurses can fix it, but if it still hurts later on, I'll have to call in Malakai and ask him if he can do something about it.

Anyway, mom just ordered dinner and now she's getting snippy about me being on my laptop. She wants me to use this time while I'm in the hospital to rest rather than stay on my laptop.

She was like, *"You're here to rest for your surgery, so stay off that thing unless it's for school. You hear me?"*

She didn't stutter. Plus, she probably has a point. Because I'll be missing an entire week of school, I'll be working twice as hard in order to stay caught up with my assignments. (I'll also be on edge considering who Principal Vickins assigned as my informant, so that'll be fun.)

Anyway, I should probably get some rest. I don't know what's going to happen for the rest of the week. Thanks for the support and take care.

Your Friend,

Meagan Wright

Section 4
2013-2014

SENT: January 9th, 2013

Lee,

I'm trying to find a good, creative way to start this email and nothing is really coming to mind. I was released from the hospital two days ago, and it feels good to be out of there. I was able to go back to school today and act as if things were normal.

Only thing is that I had to keep my left arm in a sling to restrain myself from lifting my arm and causing damage to my stitches. Six weeks, the doctor said. I had to wear the sling for six weeks in order for my incision to heal properly. It sucks but six weeks will fly by before I know it.

It's just hard to get dressed sometimes since it's a pain getting into my uniform shirt for school. I usually have to force my arms through the shirt with all my might since I'm real busty, but it fits perfectly below the chest area. The shirt literally flares out a bit at the bottom and stretches.

I've always had a big chest. I get it from my mom's side of the family. On my dad's side, women have big butts and thick thighs, so I deal with that too. It's nothing I can change, no matter how much I exercise. I've lost weight these past few months. I measured my waist this morning and I've lost three inches. Other than my stomach and arms, everything else stays the same.

Still have thick thigs, a big butt, and am forever busty. It's both a blessing and a curse that'll probably never change as I get older.

Anyway, when I got to school, I felt a few people staring at me but I tried not to let the feeling get to me. I arrived at school early, so I was sitting in the cafeteria until it was time for homeroom. I was listening to some music and I started sketching in my notebook. I was in the zone. I thought of a sunset settling behind a great mountain that was covered in snow. There were trees covered in snow and a small lake at the bottom, but you could see the reflection of the trees in the water.

Someone tapped my shoulder and brought me back to reality. I looked up as Benton sat beside me, a smile on his face. It took me a minute to realize it was him since his hair was cut short—it was chin-length and fell in waves.

"You lose a bet?" I asked him.

He rolled his eyes, sucking his teeth. He said his parents had been recently debating on him getting a haircut. Benton never had a problem with his hair being long, it suited him well. But he said when his grandparents visited the other day, he overheard them criticizing his parents for allowing him to grow his hair long and it sort of made him feel sick.

"They thought it was weird that my hair was so long. I think they just didn't like it, but it riled up my parents a bit. I could hear my parents talking about it. I got it cut the other day just to get some peace. I felt bad, you know?"

I honestly didn't know what to say in response. The whole thing was ridiculous. Childish, to be honest. I didn't want to seem disrespectful by telling him that his grandparents were absolute dipwads for criticizing his hair, so I kept my mouth shut. I shrugged my shoulders and rubbed his back a bit. I was tempted to run my fingers through his hair just to feel the silky texture.

Even with it short, I still liked Benton's hair. Very much.

"I like it," I told him. "This way. And the other way too."

Benton's cheeks were a soft red and he pressed his lips together in a tight grin. His eyes then drifted to my notebook and he tapped his finger on my sketch. "You drew that?" His voice was soft and he leaned over the picture, eyeing the entire page.

When I nodded, telling him, "Yeah, I did", Benton's eyes went bonkers and were so wide I thought they were going to pop right out of his head.

"You…drew *this*? Really?!"

"I just doodled a bit, nothing serious."

He snorted and snatched the notebook from under my hand. He held up the picture so I could get a look at it as he was facing me. He held the notebook against his chest with one hand, and motioned his other hand over the entire page, saying, "This! This is not doodling, it's a masterpiece!"

Benton was so loud that it kind of startled me. Usually he's so quiet, not drawing attention. I put my hand over his mouth, telling him that he was being too loud.

"Thanks, but you don't have to let the whole world know."

He lowered my hand from off his face. "Why not?" He was back to his normal, hushed voice. "The world should know."

I snorted. "You're starting to sound like Donny a bit." I caught myself. "I mean *Donald*." It wasn't really a big deal, me calling

175

Donald *'Donny'* in front of other people, but it didn't feel right to call him that when he wasn't around.

Speaking of which, Donny wasn't in school today. Neither was Moe. I probably shouldn't have been surprised when I didn't see them at all. It had been a while since I had heard from Donny. I figured he was done with me after our last conversation, but I didn't want to let that get to me. I wanted to think things were going to get better. But I was still a bit unsure, you know?

I was on my way to first period when I thought about sending Donny a text to let him know that I missed talking to him, and I wanted him to know that I cared about him. I really did miss him. That stupid, cheeky smirk of his. The way he would always click his tongue and wink whenever he was trying to be a smartass. The way he kept his hair slicked back without using an excessive amount of hair gel. I missed when he would throw his arm around me without warning. I missed his ridiculous laugh that would sometimes make me laugh, and the way his nose would wrinkle as he laughed. Most of all, I missed the sound of his voice—hearing him call me *'kid'*.

I missed all of him. All the ridiculous and tolerable things about him. I missed it. So I thought, *Screw it*, and I sent him a text. I kept it brief so I didn't seem overbearing.

- **Hey Donny. I just wanted to see how you've been. Things have been busy lately but I want you to know that I'm always here for you and that you matter to me. Love you.**
Short and sweet.

As I hit send, someone bumped into my left arm and I whipped my head around to get a look at the person. I saw Nathan

Hendricks staring back at me with his lips slightly parted open.

Oh crap, oh crap, oh crap, was all I kept thinking to myself as he looked at me.

"Sorry, Meagan. I didn't see you there. You okay?" He was genuinely concerned, I could tell. Probably because of my arm.

I cleared my throat and fixed the bookbag strap on my right arm. I could only use my right arm for everything since my left arm was in a sling, so you can imagine how much strength that took.

I told Nathan that I was fine and he let out a sigh.

"I can carry that for you if you'd like," he offered.

"Nah, it's okay."

"C'mon, it's no big deal. Your class is down the hall and I can tell that's weighing you down a bit I bet. It's the least I could do. Plus, technically, I am still kinda your informant until the end of the week, so."

(Oh yeah, Nathan was my informant while I was out of school during my surgery. Such a coincidence. Although, to be honest, he was a good informant. Whenever he would visit me to give me my assignments, he would sit with me for a bit in case I had any questions. He didn't have to do that, but he did it anyway. My mom actually liked having him around, and soon enough, I kind of did too. We would sometimes talk about things that didn't involve school, like books and movies. It was nice.)

Without warning, Nathan slipped the strap of my bookbag off my shoulder and carried my bookbag in his hand. He gestured for me to lead the way to my first period class.

"Right behind you," he said, arching an eyebrow with one

corner of his mouth curved upward in a smirk.

He just wouldn't give up. If he hadn't been trying to act so cute, I actually would've been a little less annoyed.

Anyway, Nathan walked with me into Mr. Enrique's class and put my bookbag down beside my desk. I could feel everyone staring at us and my palms were starting to warm up. I noticed a few people whispering things to each other, and then they quickly looked away when I spotted them.

I jumped when I felt Nathan's hand rest on my shoulder. I looked up and his eyes sort of glistened from the sunlight piercing through the window.

"You all good to go?" he asked, a warm smile on his face.

I nodded. "Sure, yeah."

He then leaned forward and whispered in my ear, "The more you show you're nervous, the more they'll talk. Let them think whatever. They mean nothing, alright?"

I took a deep breath and nodded. I felt myself starting to relax as I slid into my seat. Nathan was leaving the classroom as Mr. Enrique was coming in. It was kind of funny to see them practically bump into each other.

Usually, Mr. Enrique gets pissed when students who aren't in his class are in his classroom, but he didn't mind Nathan swinging by since Nathan explained that he was helping me carry my belongings. I even vouched for him. Mr. Enrique gave him a pass and told Nathan to get to his class. I also think that if Nathan didn't have an explanation for being in Mr. Enrique's classroom,

Mr. Enrique would've given Nathan a pass anyway since Nathan was one of his best students. (That's what I heard.)

I think it's pretty funny how a lot of people liked Nathan more than Donny. Sometimes, they are the exact same person. (I only say that because I've gotten to know Nathan more while he was my informant. So in a lot of ways, he and Donny are alike.)

But like Moe said, no one thinks of brain power when people think of Donald Gonzalez. It's a shame.

The day felt slow. I did all I could to not fall asleep in any of my classes. Not because I was tired but because I was bored. Usually my teachers are engaging but today felt different. Everything was going downhill and I just couldn't stand it. I was actually looking forward to lunch but I wasn't able to go to lunch with my friends since I was scheduled for a counseling session with Counselor Rashad, which I didn't find out until the very last minute.

I was literally on my way to lunch, and I just so happened to bump into Counselor Rashad in the hallway. He said that he was looking forward to our counseling session.

"I'll see you in ten minutes," he said before heading upstairs to his office. I was pissed. No one told me about this.

I figured Principal Vickins had something to do with this.

Who else?

There was no need for me to have a session with Counselor Rashad, it was all BS. I'm not saying that Counselor Rashad sucks at his job, he's a great counselor, but the session was pointless. At least to me. He asked about my day so far and wanted to know how my classes were going. I told him that everything was fine and that my classes were fine too.

"I'm aware Nathan Hendricks was chosen to be your informant during your absence. How was he?"

"He was fine. Reliable. Nice to be around."

Counselor Rashad chuckled. "Well we do try to select the best for the best." *Of course y'all do.*

I was relieved when the bell sounded, signaling the end of the lunch period, which also meant the end of my counseling session. I couldn't get out of there fast enough.

Again, it's nothing against Counselor Rashad because once upon a time, I needed those counseling sessions.

But now I don't anymore. The worst part is that no one even told me that I was signed up for a session. I had to find out from Counselor Rashad himself that we had a session.

It's ridiculous.

When school was over for the day, I was overjoyed. It felt like literal hell, and I was so ready to get out of there.

Right after school, we all went over Christopher's place to hang out—me, Peter, Carmen, and Benton. Christopher's dad wasn't home from work yet, so Christopher told us we could chill in the living room. Usually we're in the basement whenever Christopher's dad is home. Even though Christopher lives in a big nice, his dad didn't like Christopher having a lot of people over.

It's pretty fun though since his dad didn't seem to mind us being over when we were helping Christopher clear out the garage a few weeks ago.

The four of us watched a movie that Peter picked out from the basement called *Time Dimension Warp*. It's about these two boys, Jaime and Oliver, who invent a time machine in the form of a stopwatch in order to prevent the First World War but end up in 1780 during the American Revolution. It's a cult classic that perfectly showed the many wonders of CGI and redefined teen movies during the '80s, making it one of the greatest films in history.

But it didn't really surprise me that Benton's never seen *Time Dimension Warp* before since he's still a little uncultured. When Peter made a reference from the movie, Benton's eyebrows furrowed in confusion and Peter shook his head.

"*Ay Dios mío!* What world do you live in?" he groaned.

Fortunately, Benton Son's days of pop-culture negligence were over.

As all of us were watching *Time Dimension Warp*, Benton was so engrossed in the movie. He sat in the same position with his arms folded and his legs crossed for almost two hours. I couldn't take my eyes off him. He would smile occasionally at some parts but kept a straight face throughout the rest of the movie.

Once it was over, Benton had a ton of questions, which was expected since the movie ended on a major cliffhanger. Hence there being a sequel, which was even more successful than the first film. I was sure Christopher had the sequel, but we weren't able to watch it since it was getting late. Christopher's dad was probably heading home from work, and we didn't want Christopher to get in trouble for having us over, so we had to head home.

Benton and I had no problems catching the bus home. While we were on the bus, Benton just kept going on and on about the movie, sharing all types of theories and asking so many questions. I should've been annoyed but I wasn't. I thought it was adorable. He was like, "So does the amulet on the stop-watch mean something? And did Jaime purposely send them to the wrong time period? I think he did. Maybe not but I think so."

He had so much enthusiasm, and he was so anxious from the suspenseful ending. I could tell it was killing him.

I told him, "The second movie answers most of your questions, but I still don't know about Jaime. They never addressed whether he did it on purpose or not."

Benton let out a sigh in astonishment.

The bus pulled up to our stop and we got off and walked the rest of the way home. We started talking about our classes and he told me about a test he had coming up for psychology. I always think it's funny when he worries himself to death over his test grades since he always scores no lower than a 95, but I guess perfection is his standard.

"Is psychology the only class that you have tests for?" I asked him, followed by a chuckle. "Or does Missus Castello just love throwing you guys tests every single day or something?"

Benton snorted, a slight grin on his face as he looked downward. "I guess she just loves challenging us more, maybe."

I'm also guessing that Mrs. Castello was fond of Benton. He was smart, so I'm sure she expected much from him and got a kick out of seeing him flex his intelligence. He aces every assignment, and it's not just for her class either. So, he's fine. I don't get why he's stressing all the time.

Anyway, mom wasn't home from work yet when I got home. I made myself a ham sandwich for dinner and did my homework after I was done eating. I received a text message from Benton while I was working on my assignment for Mr. Rover's class, and I snorted when I read the message. It was a GIF of a man stepping out into the street and flipping off a bus driver heading his way. Benton sent a follow-up text, saying: **I'm at this point rn...**

I chuckled. I could relate. I was so over my assignments for the night. I was more sick of doing homework for Mr. Rover's class than for Mr. Enrique. I was actually starting to get the hang of things for Mr. Enrique's class since Donny would always help me whenever we did homework together. He'd break things down better and made the methods seem less complicated.

I don't know how, but he did. He always did.

I then checked my phone to see if Donny had responded to my message and nothing new came up from him. My message was delivered, but that was all.

I'm probably kidding myself.

I didn't want to dwell on it, so I tried listening to some music to clear my head.

Your Friend,

Meagan Wright

Lee,

I don't know to start this email. I don't even know how I expect myself to even write this out.

The past couple of days have been somewhat tormenting, and lately I've been trying to not point out all the faults of things. But the past couple of days have been nothing but awful. I thought I was in a nightmare and I was ready to open my eyes, but there was some type of force preventing me from waking up.

I threw up a few times this week. It wasn't because I was sick, it was because of everything that was going. From school and among other things. I'd wake up in the middle of the night, run to the bathroom in the basement so my mom couldn't hear me, and I'd hurl. Sometimes, it would be impossible for me to go back to sleep afterwards. I would be up for the rest of the night and get headaches throughout the day.

It's not like it all happened without reason. There is a reason. Let me explain.

A few days ago, I was downtown with Christopher, helping him find a birthday present for Carmen. Her birthday was about a month away, but he wanted to get her something she really wanted before it was gone. She didn't directly tell him what she wanted, but he figured it was something she'd like—a necklace, I think.

Yeah, it was a necklace.

So, we get to the store and he found the perfect necklace for her. It was a really nice necklace, and it was marked down, so it was affordable. The lady who was ringing up the necklace for him had asked him if it was for someone special.

Christopher scratched the back of his head while chuckling. "You could say that, yeah." He was blushing like crazy.

I started to put the pieces together, but I didn't want to just assume that he and Carmen were probably seeing each other. So, I asked him as we were leaving the store if they were going out. Christopher looked down at the ground and crooked his lips into an awkward smile.

I heard him mutter, "Yeah", and it took everything in me to not scream out in sweet relief. It was about damn time!

I told him that too. I literally said, "It's about damn time!", and he chuckled. He said that he and Carmen decided to give things a shot around Christmas break but they were taking things slow.

"She's still getting used to dating again and I want her to be as comfortable as possible. I flat-out told her that I wouldn't be perfect right off the bat, but I'll do everything I can to make this work. If she's scared, I'll hold her hand. If she's angry at me, I'll hold her tight. No matter what, I'll do what I can for her."

He meant every word of what he said. I'll give it a month or two when he tells her that he loves her. I'm sure she'll accept it too. She probably loves him already, but she just doesn't know it.

I was happy for them. Really, I was.

"Proud of you," I said to him. "You deserve something great."

He smirked.

It didn't really surprise me that a lot happened over the break and while I was in the hospital.

Christopher asked about my surgery and how things went. He felt bad for not visiting, but things weren't going so smoothly for him and he didn't want me to worry. I told him that things went well (obviously) and that I wasn't upset with him for not visiting.

That's when I asked him, "What was going on at the time if you don't mind me asking?"

Christopher's body sort of stiffened and he looked away from me. His eyes were a little glossy and he started biting his lips.

He was nervous.

When I asked him if he was alright, he stopped walking. He looked around at the people walking by, and he finally shifted his attention back to me. I felt my heart pound heavily in my chest as he started talking to me. It was hard for him to keep his voice straight. No matter how many times he cleared his throat to get himself together, the words just wouldn't come out clear. And with his thick Irish accent on top of it, it was hard to make out some of what he was saying.

He started talking about Moe.

At first, he said that she just wasn't doing well with herself. She started getting severely depressed and wouldn't talk to anyone. She wouldn't even come out of her room to eat. She would just lay in bed for days, not saying a word to anyone. He said that when he visited her, she didn't look like herself. It was as if all the life had been sucked out of her but she was still breathing, he said.

A few days go by, and he gets a phone call from Mrs. Gonzalez. A call about Moe being dead. She didn't give him much detail but she told him that the cause was from an overdose.

Donny was the one who found her, Mrs. Gonzalez told him. Moe was tucked in bed as if she was just sleeping, but there were a few pills in her hand and she wouldn't wake up when he tried to get her up.

Christopher didn't want to believe it at first, but he knew Mrs. Gonzalez wouldn't call him unless it was something serious. So it had to be true. But not even I want to believe that it is true.

I thought I was going to vomit right where we were standing. I just felt a burning sensation in my throat and nothing came up. I didn't know what to think or say. I forgot that we were standing outside of a convenience store, and I was blocking the doorway.

I moved out the way, still trying to process everything Christopher had told me. I took huge breaths to make sure I was breathing since I felt some type of pressure on my face, but it was all in my head. I could feel Christopher's hand on my back and he was saying something to me but I couldn't really hear what he was saying. I zoned out, I guess.

I pulled out my phone and scrolled to the recent messages between me and Moe. It was on the 29th of December—not that long ago. When I spoke to her on the phone before then, she sounded fine. She wasn't hyperactive, but she didn't sound as though she was lying on her deathbed.

I almost dropped my phone but I caught it. I slipped the phone back into my coat pocket. When I looked up at Christopher, he

187

was telling me to take slow breaths and I did.

Christopher could hardly look me in the eyes. There was so much guilt hammering down on him, I thought he was going to break at any moment. All this time I was thinking she was at home, fine, but instead she's—they say she's dead, but I can't picture it.

For all I know, Moe is probably out somewhere, singing her favorite songs as loud as possible while walking around the block. Heck, she's probably getting a crème shake from Kenny's Dine-n-Dash while Donny sits in the car, waiting for her to finish up her shake.

That's how I pictured Morris-Lina Gonzalez. Off doing her thing as usual. Not in some morgue or wherever they decided to put her.

I asked Christopher if he could take me home. It was only like four-something, I think, but I used the *"my mom wants me to be home by a certain time on the weekend"* card. He probably knew I was lying, but he still took me home.

I don't remember much once he dropped me off at my house. I probably went to bed early and missed out on dinner. That's been happening a couple times, actually.

I'd come home from school and knock out my homework and go to bed without eating. I'd set my alarm so I could take my medicine but that was about it. I felt bad a couple times because mom would text me, asking what I wanted for dinner, and I would tell her that it didn't matter. She would want to sit with me and talk about my day, but I would be asleep by the time she'd get home.

I wanted to sit with her and talk to her. I just couldn't look my mother in the eyes and tell her that my friend was dead. She'd ask all sorts of questions: *"How do you know?", "Who told you?", "When did it happen?", "Are you okay?"*

I wasn't in the mood for questions. Let's be real, I'm never in the mood for questions. It's my mother though, and believe me, I feel awful. I just wanted to deal with this alone. Although, knowing my mother, she'd get worried and force me to open up about things.

I couldn't let that happen.

So yesterday and today, I started having dinner with her again, and we would talk. If school was mentioned, I'd play it off and tell her that nothing interesting happened. So far, she hasn't asked about my friends and I'm okay with that. I think I'm okay with it.

I've been trying to take things day by day. I think I'll be okay when I go to bed tonight. I threw up last night but I should be okay tonight. I try not to look at my phone before going to bed because I know I'll end up scrolling through the messages between me and Moe, and then I'll feel sick again.

So many times I wanted to reach out to Donny. Not text him. I wanted to call him to hear his voice. I can't do it now because it's late and he's probably asleep. I should probably get some sleep too. G'night.

Your Friend,

Meagan Wright

Lee,

I went over Donny's house yesterday after school. I didn't call him and give him a heads up. It probably wasn't a smart move, but I figured he probably wouldn't answer if I had called him.

I had asked Christopher, Peter, Benton, and Carmen during lunch yesterday if either one of them had heard from Donny lately. Peter told me that he ran into Donny the other day at the grocery store, but they didn't talk to each other.

"I looked at his eyes," he said. "It's always the eyes that give things away, you know."

Christopher rolled his eyes. "So does body language."

Peter shrugged. "Well, yeah, but you know the saying, *The eyes know it all and hold it all*. Am I wrong?"

No one actually says that, only he does.

But I was sort of relieved to hear that Donny wasn't just cooped up in his room. He was actually going out, although he's missed more days of school than I can count with my fingers. I'm pretty sure Principal Vickins was made aware of his situation and assigned someone to be his informant during his absence.

(Carmen told me that Principal Vickins had permission from the parents to announce Moe's death to the school the week it was confirmed. Yet, no one did anything special for her, which wasn't a surprise. Although, Donny would've scolded them if they had tried to do something special for Moe since he figured it wouldn't have

190

been genuine. It would've been out of pity and obligation by the principal.)

So right after school, I took the bus to Donny's place and once I got there, I noticed that the garage was open again. No one was in the garage, but the hood of Donny's car was lifted up. I figured he was probably still working on his car. He probably just left it alone to give himself a break.

I rang the doorbell and knocked on the door. When the door opened, I thought my heart going to pierce right out of my chest. Donny stood there—his dark hair ruffled, face fresh from a nice shave, eyes gleaming from the sunlight, and his white tank top fitting on him loosely with the hem falling over his sweatpants.

He didn't say anything at first. He just stared at me for about a minute, probably taking in the fact that I was standing at his doorstep.

I probably should've called him first. It probably wouldn't have been as awkward if I gave him the heads up. Then again, he's been shutting me out so much, not calling was probably the only option I had in order to actually see him.

By the way he was looking at me, I figured he was upset with me for just showing up unannounced. I took his silence as a sign for me to leave. Yet, to my surprise, he didn't want me to leave.

As I was turning to walk away, he reached for my wrist to stop me from leaving. When I looked at him, he let me go and shifted to the side for me to come inside.

I watched as Donny closed the door behind me and he leaned back against the wall with his arms crossed over his chest. I sat in one of the lounge chairs by the steps and I could still feel his gaze on me. The fact that he was so quiet is what really had me on edge.

I couldn't tell what he was thinking. Was he happy to see me? Was he pissed? Upset?

I opened my mouth to ask him how he was doing, which was probably a dumb question anyway, and he cut me off before I could say anything.

The first words out of his mouth were, "What are you doing here, Meagan?"

Not *"Hi"* or *"How are you?"*.

What are you doing here?, is what he asked me.

It kind of hurt, hearing that come from him. I haven't seen or heard from him in a while, and that's what he decides to say to me? It was as if he was trying to add more salt to the wound.

It was becoming difficult for me to look him in the eyes. I had a feeling that if I looked at him any longer, I'd burst into tears. It also didn't help that he kept his eyes on me as I tried to think of a response to his question. I didn't want to sound pathetic, but at the same time, it didn't matter how I wanted to sound.

I finally told him, "I just wanted to see you", and I felt a ball form in my throat. I blinked my eyes a couple times to make sure I wouldn't cry. My cheeks were starting to feel warm as the ball in my throat kept getting bigger and bigger.

I cleared my throat. "I know about Moe, so I wanted to see you. I've been wanting to see you before then too. I've just been too scared or nervous, I guess? I don't know, but that's no excuse." It felt like I was digging a hole for myself.

Donny didn't say anything at first. He walked into the kitchen and came back, offering me a water bottle. He then pulled up one of the lounge chairs and sat across from me.

After I took a sip of water from the bottle, I dared myself to look him in the eyes again. I now realized why some people thought he was intimidating. I felt myself shrinking the longer we held eye contact. I had to look away again.

Suddenly, I felt his hand over mine. For a millisecond, every bodily function had shut down and I felt my nerves spike almost instantly. I still found it hard to look him in the eyes, and then he spoke to me with his voice sounding shaky.

"I've thought about you too. A lot. Hell, I wanted to call you up the other night, but it's because I wanted to see you that I couldn't let you see me. It sounds like bullshit but with everything going on, it was the best thing, I guess."

For a second, I thought he was going to start crying but he didn't. Donny doesn't cry. At least not in front of people. But I knew he probably wanted to cry. He probably wanted to let it all out and ball his eyes out. I could tell from the sound of his voice. He was trying to suppress his emotions in order to stay strong and seem fine. He wasn't fine. He probably wanted to seem fine for my sake, but everyone has a breaking point—even tough wise-guys like Donald Gonzalez.

I let out a sigh. "It's not bullshit," I told him. "You suck at bullshitting anyway."

He snorted. "It's not that I suck at it, I just choose not to do it."

I felt more relaxed when I heard him laugh a little. I was able to look him up at him again. I wanted to reach out and wrap my arms around him. He already knew that I missed him, but just saying it wasn't enough. Yet, as much as I wanted to hug him and let him hold me in return, I had to tell myself to cool it.

I didn't want to ruin the moment by being extra.

I cleared my throat and sat up in the chair.

"I'm sorry about Moe."

He didn't scorn me for bringing it up, but I could tell it bothered him a little bit. I tried telling him that I was sorry for bringing it up but he shook his head, saying it was fine.

"It's fine, kid. I promise."

"It really isn't."

"Look, the day you actually strike a nerve, I'll let you know. Until then, we're fine. I promise." He meant every word and I was able to relax again.

He said that he's been receiving messages from everyone about Moe. From people at school to family friends and neighbors. I could tell he was getting sick and tired of it, but he couldn't say anything about it. It's normal for people to feel sorry about things like that. People dying, I mean. He just accepts whatever they have to say about it. He takes their sympathy and tells them, *"thank you"*, because that's all he can really do without seeming like a douche.

People think badly of him already.

To be honest, I doubt he'll be back at school any time soon. Knowing the delinquents of our school, they'll probably hover over him, constantly reminding him that his sister is gone and they have one less Gonzalez to deal with.

194

I hear the way people talk about them. I'm always so close to knocking someone's teeth down their throat, but I know my mom will be disappointed in me if I did. When I meet with Counselor Rashad once a week for our sessions, I want to tell him about the things people would say about Moe.

But what could he do? Call them up and give them a warning? What's that gonna do?

Honestly, I didn't blame Donny if he didn't come back to school for a while. But he had to graduate, so he would have to come back eventually. It'll only be a matter of time when Principal Vickins calls his house and tells him he has to come back or else he couldn't graduate.

There was a sudden knock at the front door, bringing us both out of our thoughts. Donny answered the door and the voice that followed sounded familiar. I saw Christopher stepping in with a bouquet of flowers. Donny shook his head, swearing.

Christopher explained to Donny that the flowers were actually from one of the neighbors. She just handed them to Christopher as he was walking up the steps. "It was an old lady in a tracksuit. I couldn't just turn her away." Christopher handed Donny the bouquet, letting out a sigh. "You gotta admit they're pretty nice though. Lilacs."

Yeah, they were nice.

Donny shrugged and set the flowers on the table in the lounge room. Christopher noticed me standing off to the side and pressed his lips together in a weak smile. He then looked back at Donny, shaking Donny's hand and pulled him in for a brief hug.

"You okay mate?" Christopher asked, followed by a sigh.

Donny's face flushed and he let out a sharp breath.

He was tired of people asking him that, I bet. He was probably tired of people wanting to check up on him.

Still, at the same time, I could tell he missed us. He really did. I mean, he told me how much he wanted to see me. But he wasn't used to this kind of attention—especially from people who wouldn't pay him any mind before.

Donny responded, "I'm still breathing, so it's a start."

Christopher rocked on his heels, nodding. That's not usually the answer you hope for, but in this case, it was good enough.

"Well, I'm not gonna hold you. I promised Pete I'd help him and his mom pull up some weeds in their garden. I just wanted to stop by and see ya."

"Appreciate it, bro." Donny shook Christopher's hand.

Christopher nodded and looked at the both of us. "I'll see you guys around." He was then out the door.

I thought it was best for me to head out too since it was getting late. It's bad enough that I didn't text my mom where I was after school. To tell you the truth, I thought she was going to ground me for life when I got home. Instead, she just told me to get changed for dinner. I didn't want to talk to her about today, though. Even when she asked about my day, I told her the usual: *nothing happened*. As if.

Your Friend,

Meagan Wright

Lee,

I had my counseling session with Counselor Rashad today during lunch, and I was honestly thinking of ditching since I didn't feel like talking. All we ever do is talk. I get that's the point of the sessions, but what if I didn't want to talk? It probably wasn't too late for me to opt out of these sessions if I wanted to.

Even if I wanted to, I couldn't without approval from the principal. It's because of Principal Vickins that I have to go to these sessions in the first place.

I can't remember if I said this before, but my dislike for the counseling sessions has nothing to do with Counselor Rashad. He's good at his job. No one could ever replace him or Counselor Malik, and I mean no one. But I didn't like spending an hour, talking about things that probably wouldn't matter in the next five or ten years.

I liked writing and doodling and reading. Those three things always made me feel better. Talking only makes things worse depending on the circumstance. But what I thought didn't matter. It feels like it sometimes doesn't matter.

So anyway, Counselor Rashad asked me about my day, as usual, and I told him that things were fine. I told him that my classes were going well and that was all. He just nodded and kept his eyes on me.

"Anything else?" he asked, taking off his glasses and setting them on his desk. I felt my chest tighten as he sat back in his seat, looking straight at me. When I shrugged my shoulders and told him that I didn't know what he meant, he was unconvinced.

It was obvious that I didn't want to be there, and Counselor Rashad pointed that out to me. He said, "I know you didn't sign up for this willingly. Maybe not at all. But still, you're here for a reason. Now, whether or not you wanna address the reason, it's up to you. Or I could address it for you."

That sick feeling in my stomach started to bubble up again as I looked at him. He and I have been at this for weeks, and I've always told him things I wanted him to hear because I thought it was easier that way. He's never complained about it before, and now all of a sudden it's a problem. It took everything in me to not get up and walk out the office.

I sat there, looking right back at Counselor Rashad as he waited for me to say something. I wanted to, so badly, but every time I opened my mouth, nothing would come out.

What was there to say? I didn't even know why I was signed up for these sessions. No one ever told me why. No one ever tells me anything. I always have to find things out by chance. It's never out of consideration.

So what could I say in response to him? More nonsense? I was already on thin-ice and I didn't want to make it worse.

Counselor Rashad suddenly asked me, "You don't know why you're here, do you?"

I was honest with him because, at this point, I was just over everything. I was tired of the bullshit, and I was tired of these sessions. I told him that I didn't even know that I was signed up for sessions until he told me himself. The only reason why I'd show up was because he would always expect me to show up, and if I tried to ditch, I would've probably regretted it.

The look on Counselor Rashad's face said it all. He didn't feel guilty. He was bothered that I didn't even know why I was attending these sessions in the first place. He thought, like I did, that someone would've said something to me in the first place. But no one told me anything. No one except him.

He rubbed his eyes, letting out a deep sigh. He then offered me a peppermint square and I took one from the jar. I played around with the wrapper after I popped the candy in my mouth. It was probably annoying the hell out of him, but he didn't say anything. Instead, he put his glasses back on and looked down at the clipboard in his hands.

Counselor Rashad then asked me, "You're aware of what happened to Morris-Lina Gonzalez, right? She's a senior. Her brother is—"

"—Donald Gonzalez. Yes. I'm aware of what was said about her." I didn't want to hear about that again. It's bad enough other students wouldn't let it go anytime she was mentioned in their conversations. I don't even know why her name would come out of their mouths. The people who talked about her didn't like her anyway.

Counselor Rashad cleared his throat and sat up in his seat. He said that when the school made the announcement about Moe, it was brought to their attention that I was a friend of hers, and so,

Principal Vickins thought it would be a good idea for me to receive counseling in order to properly cope.

I felt the sensation of peppermint burn in my throat and my eyes watered. Counselor Rashad offered me a tissue, thinking I was going to cry, but I told him that it was just the taste from the peppermint square.

I then asked him, "Who told you that we were friends?", and he told me that he couldn't disclose that information. He didn't even bat an eyelash when he said it.

Well, whoever told him that Moe and I were friends was right.

I was a friend of hers. Probably not the best friend, but I tried to be a good one. I cared about her, a lot.

Donny wasn't the only one that wanted the best for her. I did too. We all did. But she was a damn good friend herself. That's why when Christopher told me what happened, I couldn't believe it. I mean, yes, I did listen to him, but that doesn't mean I wanted to believe him.

I couldn't picture Moe being depressed out of the blue and not wanting to talk to anyone. The Morris-Lina Gonzalez I knew would never push people away. She screams attention. She'll dance in the mall to whatever song is playing and sing her heart out, annoying Donny as he tries to get her to shut up. The Morris-Lina Gonzalez I knew would never think of checking out of here before having the chance to actually live her life. If Moe ever felt upset about something, she'd reach out to me and ask if we could hang out or just talk on the phone about whatever was on her mind.

Why would she want to take the permit option to something temporary? She'd never do that. She wouldn't.

She shouldn't have.

But she did. And I wanted to know why. I needed to know why. Why didn't she call me more when she was feeling upset? The night we talked on the phone, why didn't she tell me right then and there that things weren't so good?

If not me, then why not Donny? Christopher? Carmen? Peter? Why not any of us?

I read the last text message I received from Moe to Counselor Rashad, hoping that he'd give me some type of explanation as to why she did what she did. I told him that I've read the message a million times to myself, but I still couldn't figure out why she would end things the way she did. He and I both knew that she didn't have to do what she had done, but not even he could tell me why.

Counselor Rashad handed me a tissue to wipe the tears from my eyes, and then he moved his chair around his desk so he was sitting right across from me. I knew he wasn't going to give me the answer that I wanted to hear, but I knew he was right.

He said, "As much as we want to know the real '*why*', it's not for us to know. The only one who knows that is her. I can tell she had a lot of love for you. But no one, not even her own family, will ever know why she did it. I can't speak for the dead, but Morris-Lina was good. Based on what I know of her, she was all about people living to the fullest. So, try thinking about that rather than all the things we can't explain."

Like I said, I knew he was right.

I can see Moe looking at me now, shaking her head, telling me to get my head out the gutter. She'd probably make some horrible joke that would make me laugh anyway, and then she'd throw her arm around me with that big smile of hers on her face.

It was easier to think of her being like that—the way I've always known her. The girl I met earlier in the year, feigning a terrible English accent, insisting for me to call her 'Moe', claiming that it was non-negotiable.

It's definitely better to think of her that way.

At the end of our session, Counselor Rashad said that he would talk to Principal Vickins about withdrawing me from future counseling sessions, but I told him not to bother. I could tell it caught him by surprise when I told him never mind. To tell you the truth, I sort of surprised myself. I wasn't really using my head earlier, I guess, and I sort of felt bad for disregarding how patient he's been with me all this time.

If anything, Counselor Rashad could've easily suggested for me to switch over to Counselor Malik to make it easier on himself.

And yet, he didn't. Maybe he was just trying to do his job, or maybe he actually cared. Maybe both.

I remember leaving his office and I looked down at my phone right before the bell sounded. I wanted to look at Moe's message one last time before I put my phone away for the day. I wanted to picture her saying those words to me one last time, but actually face-to-face. As I walked up to my fifth period class, I thought about her walking up with me, telling me that everything was going to be alright.

I would try to believe her.

Then I started thinking about Donny. I wondered if he thought the same thing. I wondered if he pictured Moe telling him that things were going to be okay. Even though I saw him the other day, I couldn't really tell what was going on in his head. I didn't know if he was starting to accept everything that happened, or if he was in as much denial as I had been. But him remaining in denial would've been impossible with all the condolences his family has received for the past couple of weeks.

I thought about seeing him again after school. I probably wouldn't have went over to his house, though. Instead, I would've called him, asked him if he wanted to meet up at Red Pepper's or somewhere downtown. That would've been nice, but instead, I had to go home. Unlike last time, I texted my mom that I was on my way home right after school. Then, once I walked up to the house, I sent her a text, letting her know that I was home.

As I walked up the porch steps, I saw Roselle pulling into the driveway of her house. When she got out of the car, she looked over to me and I felt my body stiffen. I could feel her scowl while she remained across the street, and yet, I still had the courage to wave to her. Just to be polite, I guess. Even if she didn't like me very much, I wanted her to realize that I really did care about Benton. I wasn't going to lead Benton on, or ditch him.

I guess she was finally starting to realize that because she eventually waved back to me before going into her house. I let out a sigh of relief. My body started to relax as I went into my house.

I had dinner ready for when mom came home so she wouldn't have to make anything. I made her favorite dish— pasta pie. Although, she sent me a message as I was cooking, telling me that she was going to be late getting home. I text her back, telling her to be safe when coming home. I wrapped up her plate of food and put it in the microwave for her to warm up when she got home. I left her a note on the microwave to let her know that her plate was already made.

After I finished eating, I cleaned the kitchen and did my homework. Mr. Rover had assigned everyone in my class to write a personal reflection essay on their progress so far, both personally and academically. He said that he wanted us to look deep within ourselves, and figure out what more we could do to improve ourselves as writers and as individuals.

He's probably been wanting to give us this assignment for a while. He sounded so serious as he explained the premise of the paper to us. It's due in about three weeks, so I'm sure it requires a lot of self-reflecting in order to impress him. Even though he never specified how long the paper had to be, I'm positive he doesn't want something less than two pages. So yeah, it's going to take more than just winging it. It'd probably be easier for me to write if it were just a story.

Your Friend,

Meagan Wright

Lee,

The past couple of days have been exhausting. My brain has been tormented with boatloads of assignments while trying to function on little to no amount of sleep. Fortunately, I was able to sleep-in this weekend to give my body some rest. So for the first time in a while, I was able to go through the whole day of school without feeling like a zombie.

Although, I wish I had been a zombie because maybe Preston wouldn't have asked me to help him recruit more people for the theater program interest meeting. (Turns out the first interest meeting was a fluke, so Dexter wanted to try for a second one, and he put Preston in charge of recruitment. Hardly shocking at all.)

Then again, Preston didn't really ask me. He more so pulled me aside during homeroom and was like, "Hey, in between class periods, you're helping me recruit people. Now go."

So, basically, I didn't have much of a choice.

Preston and I walked up and down the halls, trying to get students to sign up for the interest meeting. We hardly had any luck. Preston was approaching people left and right before going to his next class, and I even tried recruiting people right before my classes started. I managed to get one girl to sign up from my math class, but that was about it.

Preston and I met up again before lunch and he managed to get a good amount of people to sign up. I'm talking like six or seven people. That's better than me. He thought that I would probably have better luck trying to approach a group since it would lead to a possible domino effect—if one signs up, they all sign up. It usually works.

Preston spotted a couple of people from the lacrosse team just hanging out by the lockers. He suggested for me to go over to them. I looked and I saw Diana and Austin Brown within the group, laughing like hyenas. I snorted. There was no way I was going over there. It's not that I'm scared of them, but one look at me and they'll probably eyeball me as if I am lost. I didn't want to put up with that. Not today.

I told Preston, "I'm not doing it", and he rolled his eyes.

"Just do it. It'll help improve your people skills."

I wrinkled my eyebrows. "I have great people skills."

Preston sighed, rubbing his eyebrows. "People who have great people skills are usually well-liked, and I can honestly tell you, five out of the seven days of the week, I hardly like you. So just go." He nudged me forward a little and I swatted at his arm.

I told him that if he was so confident in his people skills, he should be the one to go over and talk to them. The look on Preston's face was priceless. He probably thought I hit my head on a rock or something. He came up with all sorts of excuses as to why he couldn't go over and talk to them. One of the reasons had involved Erik Petrov. I didn't think anything of it at first when he pointed out Erik as one of the reasons.

Then it hit me.

"You like him, don't you?"

Preston gave me a stern look. I tried to hide my face with the clipboard but it hardly helped. Preston huffed, crossing his arms over his chest, tapping his foot while shaking his head.

That meant, *yes*.

Never in a million years would I have thought that Preston would like someone from the lacrosse team. It's the lacrosse team. Most of them are a-holes.

But Erik was pretty nice. I never spoke to him personally, but I would see the way he treated others. He always greets people and helps people out without being asked. He's also very a good-looking guy. Tall, tan, fit, nice hair, and light-colored eyes. He's almost as attractive as Nathan.

I just couldn't believe that Preston liked him.

I snorted. "I can't believe you like Erik Petrov."

"Yeah, well, he asked me to prom, so what're you gonna do?"

I thought my ears were playing tricks on me, but Preston repeated what he had said. I wasn't going crazy. Erik Petrov asked Preston Highmore to prom. I was practically speechless.

Anyway, Preston was still urging me to go over and try to convince them to sign up for the interest meeting. Out of nowhere, Nathan comes up to us, asking if we're alright. Preston and I were probably making huge fools of ourselves, shoving each other in the middle of the hallway.

Preston had the audacity to tell Nathan that I was the one being difficult by not talking to a few members of the lacrosse team. I was being a chicken, he said. He had some nerve.

Nathan offered to go over and talk to them but I told him that it was fine. I just decided to go over and do it. It wasn't that I had a problem with Nathan going over and talking to them, I just wanted to prove Preston wrong and show him that my people skills were pretty solid.

But I ended up making an absolute fool of myself.

I should've been smart when I went over there to them. I should've known that they would crack jokes and make me feel incompetent, but I didn't run away with my head down. I just looked at them with the clipboard to my chest.

Austin Brown was the worst of them all. He wouldn't give me a break. Every time I tried to get a word in, he had something smart to say. I imagined myself punching him in the softest spot on his body. Maybe then he would learn how to shut-up.

Out of nowhere, Nathan comes up behind me, asking if everything was alright. That's when Austin had finally shut up, but he still had a smug look on his face. Once Nathan showed up, they were all quiet. Diana looked away from him when they made eye-contact and she moved in closer to Austin.

Nathan then looked up at Austin as he gave Nathan a dirty look. Nathan just stared right back at Austin, completely unfazed. I took a few steps over to the side in case one of them decided to take the first swing.

That's usually what happens, but luckily, nothing happened. The two of them just had a little stare-down and exchanged a few words. From some of the things Nathan had said, I really thought Austin was going to deck him. I could see it in his eyes. I reached for Nathan's arm, tugging him away as the bell signaled the next class period.

Nathan kept looking back at them as we walked away. He finally gave me his attention once we were down the other end of the hall. He didn't need to step in the way he did. It was chivalrous, maybe, but he didn't have anything to prove. Not to me, not to them, to no one. Besides, if a fight had broken out, he'd be in a world of trouble.

It wouldn't have mattered who started the fight. I couldn't just let Nathan set himself up like that—it wouldn't be right.

I told him, "You're not dumb like them, so don't act dumb."

A smirk curled on his lips and I furrowed my eyebrows.

He snickered. "I never knew you cared about what happens to me," he said, stuffing his hands in his pants pocket while rocking on his heels.

I rolled my eyes, shaking my head.

He turned on his heels and started walking away. He looked back at me as he pushed open the double-doors, and he flashed a smirk. Then he was gone.

I was able to make it to my English class in the nick of time, but Mr. Rover still called me out for coming in as the second bell sounded off. He usually has the door closed before the second bell, but today, he was feeling generous.

Today, he talked more on our personal reflection essays, which are due in a few weeks. As he was talking about it, I felt my anxiety starting to spike. I honestly had no idea how I was going to pull this paper off. He wasn't looking for anything fluffy or sappy. He wanted us to be honest and really look deep within ourselves, and he wanted it to be good.

So in other words, no BS.

Mr. Rover made it perfectly clear that if we even tried to BS our way through this paper, he would know.

He was like, "I know all of you well enough, so you can try to outsmart me but you won't. At the end of the day, I get paid to teach you. So best believe I'll do all I can to make sure you learn something from this."

At the end of class, Mr. Rover asked to speak with me and I felt my heartbeat faster than a rabbit's. I told myself not to worry because I figured it was nothing bad. I've never done anything out of line, and I always turned in my assignments on time. So what would've been the problem?

He could probably tell how nervous I was as I sat down in the seat next to his desk. He offered me a peppermint square and I took one. (I feel like all the faculty members having nothing but peppermint squares because that's all anyone offers me. Even though I'm sick of them, I still take them because I know I'll feel bad if I refuse one. Plus, they are kind of addicting, and I like playing around with the wrappers. It calms my nerves.)

Mr. Rover said that he heard that I was one of the finalists in the Philadelphia School District's Annual Writers' Competition, and he's been meaning to congratulate me for a while. He's just never had the chance.

I smiled and thanked him.

He gave me a slight head nod.

Mr. Rover then asked me if I was feeling okay. He said I hardly looked focused today, but I would beg to differ.

I mean, I was fine. I was probably in a daze for a bit since I kept thinking about the personal reflection essay and how to go about it.

So I was honest with him. I told Mr. Rover how I felt about the whole thing. I told him that I honestly had no idea what to write about or how I should even start writing the paper. He was basically asking me to catch a fish without teaching me how to fish, it felt like.

I know I was probably overthinking the whole thing, but I've never written something like this before. I'm good at writing stories or prompted essays.

Not deep, thought-provoking, personal stuff.

Mr. Rover let out a sigh and told me to relax. I was worrying about nothing, he said. He believed that I was able to handle it, but at the same time, he thought I wasn't giving myself a chance to really go for it.

"I've seen your writings and yes, they are good, but they could be great. You always stay on the surface to stay safe. After a while, you'll get tired of playing it safe. You may not know it now, but soon enough you'll want to go a little farther and look deeper within yourself. You'll have to start with a little push until you finally get to that point on your own." He was giving me that push.

I know that down the line, as a writer, I'll have to shake things up a bit in order to keep people engaged. Not every story will be the same because not every story is supposed to be the same. You have to keep things fresh in order to attract different people. If you read the same thing over and over again, you'll get sick and tired of it and not want to think about it anymore.

If I didn't want that to happen to me, I had to think outside the box, which meant figuring out who I am as a writer and as a person. That's why he's giving us three weeks to complete this paper. No one can deeply figure themselves out in a day or two. It takes time, and I'm going to need a lot of time in order to make this possible.

Mr. Rover allowed me to leave since he had another class coming in. Before I left, I turned around and asked him how many pages he wanted the paper to be. He stood up from behind his desk and let out a sigh.

"No more than five hundred and no less than three," he said, clearly making a joke. Still, I nodded.

During lunch, I was jotting down ideas on what to write about. I thought about writing about my heart condition, but I didn't want to just stick with that as my default topic.

I felt someone tap my shoulder and I looked up from my notebook. Benton asked me what I was writing about and I told him about the personal reflection essay.

Peter gagged and I could see the chewed up bits of tater tots in my mouth, making me wrinkle my nose. Christopher reached over and plucked him on the neck, telling him to show a little more class.

Peter rolled his eyes. "I have class, thank you very much. I just think personal reflection is a load of bull. And to get a grade for it? *Diablo.*"

Carmen chimed in and asked me how many pages the paper

had to be. I told her the exact words Mr. Rover told me— *"no more than five hundred and no less than three"*. They all looked at me with wide eyes. They thought I was being serious. I told them it was a joke and they blinked, starting to breathe.

Peter let out a huff. "I was about to say—what the hell is up with him? Someone must've got him hooked on some funny juice because sir, that's real funny." He went back to eating his lunch and I chuckled. He grinned with a mouthful of food in his mouth and looked over at Christopher. "Ha! See, I can be funny, Chrissy."

Christopher's face went bright red and he gave Peter the most frightening scowl I've ever seen. I honestly thought he was going to wrap his fingers around Peter's neck and strangle him. Shouldn't Peter know by now to not call Christopher *'Chrissy'*?

Peter was lucky that Carmen was there, otherwise, Peter would've been a dead man. Carmen turned Christopher's head to face her and told him to let it go. Christopher kept mumbling that he was going to one day kill Peter one day. Carmen just nodded, saying things like, *"I know, I know, but you gotta love 'em anyway. We love him anyway. Relax."*

Benton asked me if I was going straight home after school and I nodded. He smirked, asking if we could walk home together. Obviously I told him that we could, I don't even know why he asked. We literally live right across the street from each other, it was no problem.

Although, it was a bit of a pain getting home once school let out. There was snow and ice everywhere, so it took a while for the bus to come pick us up from the bus stop once we got off the train. Twenty minutes had gone by and I sent a text to my mom, letting her know that I was waiting for the bus with Benton. She responded with a smiley face and a thumbs up.

"How's your mom doing?" I heard Benton ask.

I stuffed my phone in my pocket as I looked over at him.

"She's fine," I replied, sniffing from the cold air. "She's at work right now but by this time this bus comes, she'll get home before I do. It'll probably be dinner time too."

Benton softly chuckled, and all of a sudden, the bus turned the corner and started to pull up to our stop. (God answers prayer.) My fingers were numb as the warmth from the inside of the bus hit my face, sending shivers down my spine.

It was a long and bumpy ride. Benton and I managed to get off the bus okay once we came to our stop.

As we walked the rest of the way home, we started talking about our weekend plans. Benton said that his parents were going away on a little trip, so he and Roselle would have the house to themselves for the weekend. He already knew she would probably have a couple of her friends over, but he said he liked her friends.

"One of them has a funny name. *Chee-tee*, I think. He has dark blue hair but it looks nice on him."

I couldn't help but laugh as I pictured this friend of Roselle's. He seemed pretty cool the more Benton talked about him. The guy would come over and always offered Benton some chocolate candy. He'd even talk to Benton about anything that was on his mind, whether it was personal or school-related. He was like a big brother to him, Benton said.

We then talked about school, and I told Benton that I was planning on working on my personal reflection essay as soon as possible. I wanted to brainstorm some more ideas. Hopefully I would be able to come up with something that didn't just focus on my heart condition. I had to look deeper. It's just like Mr. Rover said—I can't stay on the surface forever.

Anyway, as Benton and I were walking around the corner to the next block, a bunch of middle schoolers jumped out from behind the corner gate and chased us up the block. They were hitting us with snowballs as we tried to get away from them. Some of the snowballs felt hard as ice—probably because they were ice. Benton and I were able to use our bookbags to block some of the snowballs, but a few of the middle schoolers came around us and threw some at our legs. It was painful. They finally left us alone once we made it up the block and they ran away.

Snow was all in my hair and the hood of my coat. My legs were freezing, and my arms felt sore from *iceballs*. Not snowballs, *iceballs*. Benton was trying to catch his breath and dusted the snow off of his pants and out of his hair.

"What the hell," he panted, feeling his hair.

I bet those kids were from Almech Middle School, which was a couple blocks away from where Benton and I lived. The kids at that school were always causing problems. One time, a couple of the kids from Almech tried to rob the corner store, but the owner was able to catch one of them and he called the police.

But it's like my mom always says: *it starts at home.*

Anyway, Benton and I sort of leaned on each other as we made our way up the rest of the block. It was a pain walking across the street to my house since my legs were sore. I turned on the heat as soon as I entered my house, and as I made my way up the steps to my room, I had to lean on the banister for support.

Usually ice helps, but after what happened, I wasn't icing anything. I needed something hot but we didn't have anything hot.

So I just had to tough it out and wear sweatpants and long sleeves in case I had any bruises. The last thing I wanted was for my mom to knock on every door in the area, hunting a couple of kids who ambushed her sixteen-year-old daughter with a bunch of snowballs (and iceballs).

Knowing Benton, he's probably trying to hide his pain as well. Our mothers were relentless, and we just wanted to keep the peace in the area. No trouble at all.

Your Friend,

Meagan Wright

SENT: February 5th, 2013

Lee,

This morning I woke up to the sound of my mom getting ready for work. It was maybe seven-something in the morning. At first I thought I had to get up for school. I was so used to my mom waking me up in the morning, but that's only if I slept through my alarm. But then I checked the date on my phone and the time.

It was seven in the morning on a Saturday.

Saturday, meaning that although she had to go to work, I didn't have school. So I was fine. But I just couldn't go back to sleep. I tried and I tried, but I was already awake. It was pointless.

So, I went downstairs and made myself some breakfast as my mom was heading out the door. She reminded me to do my chores before she got back home tonight. I told her that I would.

My chores are simple: mop the floors, dust the tables and the ornaments, and sweep the porch.

It usually takes me a whole day to get everything done, so I did my chores as soon as possible. Once I was finished breakfast, I mopped the floors and I dusted the tables and the ornaments.

I was in the zone. I figured that I would sweep the porch later since there wasn't much to sweep. There were a few bits of snow on the porch but it wasn't really a big deal.

I checked the time and saw that it was cutting close to 11:30 in the morning. I was covered in dust and smelled like lemons from the furniture polish. I went upstairs and took shower and changed into one of my nightshirts.

I went downstairs and adjusted the temperature of the house since I thought I was going to melt. My mom always has the heat ridiculously high whenever winter hits. Sometimes I can't even sleep because I'm sweating like a sinner in church.

Once I was comfortable, I decided to start working on my paper for Mr. Rover. I listened to some music, hoping that would give me some type of inspiration on how to start the paper. Each song was different, but nothing was coming to me.

You'd think I was brain dead.

I suddenly heard someone knock on the front door and I bolted down the steps with my phone in my hand.

I answered the door. I froze, and my phone almost slipped right out of my hand. All I saw was Donny, standing there with his hair tousled, wearing his thick black jacket over his white shirt that was tucked into his blue jeans.

Neither of us knew what to say. He probably wasn't expecting me to answer the door. I sure wasn't even expecting him to be standing at my doorstep. It wasn't like him to show up out of the blue.

He opened his mouth to speak but I could tell he was struggling to formulate his words.

I cleared my throat. "Hey." I gulped. "How are you?"

Donny ran his fingers through his hair while rocking on his heels. "I was in the area and I just—uh, well I thought I should stop by and see you." He moved to the side so I could get a look at his car, all fixed and parked in front of my house.

I pointed out the obvious. "You fixed it."

He nodded, stuffing his hands in his pants pockets. "Yeah." He started to lean off to the side but he caught himself.

I pretended not to notice, but I had to press my lips together to prevent myself from laughing. He sort of smiled and looked down at his shoes.

He cleared his throat and looked back up at me. "So what are you doing today? Like right now?"

"Nothing, just chilling." I was sick of that essay.

Donny's eyes suddenly softened and he seemed almost child-like. He inhaled and nodded his head, saying, "Okay." He looked away from me clicking his tongue. "I was only asking because I was wondering if you would want to go somewhere with me. If you want?"

"Where is it?" I asked, leaning against the doorframe.

Donny licked his lips, smirking. "It's a surprise."

"You know I don't like surprises."

"Alright then, what if I said it was one of my favorite places?"

"Where? Like how far is it from here?"

I wasn't trying to be difficult, I just wanted to know because I wanted to be back home before my mom got off of work. She would be worried sick if she came back and I wasn't home.

It's the weekend, so where would I even go?

I think Donny was finally starting to realize that and he told me that the place wasn't far. "Only a twenty minute drive if we're lucky," he said. "You'll be back before mama bear comes crawling back, I promise you."

I looked him in the eyes and I took his word for it.

So, I told him to give me twenty minutes to get changed and then we could go. He waited in his car while I got dressed. It didn't take me long to get dressed, actually. Once I was ready to go, Donny got out the car and opened the front passenger door for me. As I was settling in his car, I was starting to remember how good it felt sitting in his car. The vintage leather was firm yet smooth at the same time.

I always liked Cadillac cars, but Donny's car was different. I loved his car. When he got in and buckled up, he turned the dial to some random music station and cranked up the volume before pulling off.

Even though it was a slow drive because of the ice, it felt like we were cruising down the road without any worries. It felt better than when I rode with him in his car for the very first time. I rested my head back and closed my eyes.

I felt the car stop and I heard Donny ask me if I was alright.

I opened my eyes and saw that we were only at the first traffic light. That's when I knew that this was going to be a long ride. But I looked at Donny and told him that I was fine.

He snickered, pulling off when the light turned green. "I guess I get five stars for being the most unentertaining chauffer ever."

I snorted. "At least you know how to drive on ice, though."

You don't know how many drivers I've seen who don't know how to drive slowly on the road when it's icy. It's like they're hoping to cause an accident. It's even worse on the highway. So many people just zip through the lanes as if they're drag racing.

Luckily, Donny and I didn't encounter any hooligans on our way to one of his 'super-secret-favorite-spots'. (He didn't call it that, but he wouldn't tell me a thing about the place until we got there.)

While we're in the car, my phone buzzed in my pocket and I saw that I had a text from Nathan. (Because he was my informant, he also has my phone number, so that's a thing.) He sent me a photo of the flyer for the show we're hoping to do this year—and my God it looked awesome.

This year we're doing *Odella*, which is a musical written by Alize Lynell Wells, a famous playwriter from Sweden.

The show takes place in the early 1800s in Rome. It follows a migrant woman who seeks revenge on her late-husband's mistress, whom he had a child with. So in order to ruin the mistress's life, the woman decides to get closer to the mistress's child and then kill him.

It's a really good story and it's kind of sad too. I've only seen it once with my dad when I was younger. One of his coworkers had extra tickets, so he decided to take me to go see it since he didn't want to waste the tickets. I was probably ten-years-old, and my dad took me to see a musical that featured lust, gruesome murder, and drinking. It was my kind of show. I mean that too.

I was thrilled that we were doing *Odella* for theater.

I had such a big smile on my face, Donny started snickering. "Get a text from your boyfriend or something?"

Ha! Funny. "No," I said, wrinkling my nose. When I told him

that Nathan sent me a text about the show we're doing this year for theater, Donny's eyebrows wrinkled and his lips twisted.

"Nathan?" His head slightly jerked. "So you two are like a thing now or something?" The tone of his voice softened, and so did the look on his face as he kept his eyes forward.

"No," I replied. "He's just part of the theater program now." I watched as Donny let out a soft sigh and drummed his thumbs against the wheel. I went on, telling him that Nathan was my informant during my absence from school, and I told Donny that Nathan wasn't too bad. He was actually trying to get himself together and turn things around. Plus, he was nice to be around.

Donny didn't seem too convinced.

"Yeah, well, at least one of us can think that way about him." Judging by his tone, I thought he was going to bite my head off, and he didn't look at me once. He just kept his eyes on the road, his jaw tightening.

I reminded Donny that once upon a time, he was friends with Nathan—based on what Christopher had once said. Donny's grip tightened on the wheel and his nostrils flared. I don't know what caused him to resent Nathan so much, but people really do change if they cut the right people out of their lives. For Nathan, it was Diana, and Donny just needed to realize that, and I knew he would. He had to, eventually.

Finally, Donny sighed. "Just give me some time, kid. I get what you're saying. Don't think I don't. It's just gonna take more than him just kissing up to you for me to know for sure that he's himself turned around." This time he looked at me, but it was only for a second, and he lifted one side of his mouth into a smirk.

I nodded and said, "Okay", and that was the end of it.

He eventually pulled into an abandoned parking lot that was surrounded by nothing but trees. I started feeling uneasy as Donny parked the car, then turning off the engine. There was complete silence and it was just the two of us. The highway was far behind us. When Donny got out of the car, the coldness hit me instantly, sending shivers down my body.

I took a deep breath, puffing warm air into my cuffed hands. Donny opened my car door, gesturing for me to come out. Once I was standing outside, my eyes started to water from the harsh breeze. I had to shut my eyes at one point and I nuzzled my nose into my cotton scarf.

Donny walked around me and held out his arm.

"Madam," he said in a terrible English accent.

I snorted, locking my arm with his.

I truly despise walking in snow. Even though it looks real pretty on trees, snow is an absolute nightmare when trying to walk up and down steep hills. I had to cling onto Donny for dear life as we walked down one of the giant hills. I swear, I thought I was going to fall and crack my head open. The snow made everything ten times harder, but luckily, I didn't fall on my butt once.

If I had, Donny wouldn't let me live it down.

We eventually reached an opening, allowing us to escape out of the woods, and I was marveled at the sight. There was a lake, completely covered in ice, and on the opposite side, there was a wide open space completely covered in snow. The sky looked different on the other side. There was some blue mixed with some gray and a bit of orange from the emerging sunlight.

It was unlike anything I had ever seen.

Donny told me that when he and Moe were kids, their father would take them to the lakeside, and they would set off fireworks and watch the stars 'til midnight. As he and Moe got older, Donny would sometimes drive up to the lakeside with Moe to watch the stars and set off fireworks all through the night.

"Sometimes we'd be out so late, mom would call us, all worried and would want us to come back home." He sat down on the ground, leaning back on his elbows. There was hardly any snow near the lakeside, surprisingly. "We'd be out here for hours, just taking everything in."

I don't blame him. It was beautiful out there.

I joined Donny on the ground, pulling my knees close to my chest as his arms came around me. We stared out into the open space in absolute silence. It was like a wonderland, something straight out of a storybook—kind of like an ancient fantasy realm.

It's no wonder it was one of his favorite places.

It was starting to become mine.

Usually nothing is perfect, but this—this was close to perfect.

Suddenly, Donny tells me that Moe called the lakeside her *"safe place"*. He said every time they would go there, she would seem more free than a bird. She'd sing more, laugh more, dance more. He admitted that he would often join in with her, and they'd be restless. It was like their own kingdom, and everything else in the world no longer mattered.

He let out a soft sigh and his arms loosened from around me.

"She would've loved today," he said, sitting up. He pointed to the field on the other side of the lake. "There's never been this much snow to cover the field like that."

I shifted my gaze up to Donny. He had a slight grin on his face as he sat with his knees pulled into his chest with his arms wrapped around his legs. Something was on his mind. Probably all the memories he shared with Moe when they were younger, setting off fireworks and stargazing. He was quiet, probably forgetting that I was even there. Maybe for a second.

Then out of the blue, Donny breaks the silence and asks me, "Did I ever tell you that she was pregnant once? Morris-Lina?"

I thought I had misheard him. My eyebrows wrinkled and my lips were parted. There was no way that was possible.

Moe? Pregnant? There was no way.

"You're kidding."

"Why would I kid about that?" He was unconsciously loud and I could tell he was offended by my accusation.

I shook my head. "I'm not saying you're a liar. It's just...I can't believe it. Her being pregnant. Like, that's *huge*."

Donny snorted. "Well, it's not something you normally talk about. But do I seem like the type of person to make that shit up?"

No. He wasn't the kind of person to make up something like that. Not even as a joke. It'd be a horrible joke.

So, it was true. Moe was once pregnant.

I was not expecting that, so I didn't know what to say.

Donny started telling me the story about Moe being pregnant.

She was young, real young. They were in their freshman year, and she had been seeing a guy who was a year older. He didn't go to the same school as them. In fact, Donny wasn't sure if the guy was in school at all. She met him at the corner store and they exchanged phone numbers, Donny said.

Everything was cute at first until they started dating. Their parents didn't really like the guy since they didn't know much about him. Donny was skeptical, thinking the guy was no good and would probably up and leave Moe one day. He felt bad for thinking like that, but he had a hunch.

Then one day, Donny was in her room looking for something—he couldn't remember what exactly—but instead, he found an empty pregnancy test box on the floor of her closet. Later that same day, Moe had come home after hanging out with the guy and Donny just lost it. Not on her, but the guy. As soon as the guy pulled up to drop Moe off home, Donny bolted out of the house and started beating on the guy, practically lifting the guy out of his car.

Moe was able to pull Donny away and started yelling at him. Donny just remained focused on the guy, yelling things like, *"You knocked up my sister! You knocked up my sister!"*

Their parents weren't home at the time, so Donny felt that it was fine for him to call the guy out for what he had done. But at the same time, Moe was embarrassed. She told Donny to get a grip, saying that he was selfish for the way he acted. When she tried to talk to the guy she was seeing, he dismissed everything she said and left. He was furious because she hadn't said anything.

Turns out, she's known about her pregnancy for about a week. A week, and she didn't think to tell anyone.

Later that night, Donny went into Moe's room and spoke with her. He first apologized for the way he had acted, admitting that he could've handled things better. Moe agreed wholeheartedly. Still, she blamed herself for even getting pregnant in the first place. She didn't mean for it to happen, in fact, she didn't even want it to happen. She confessed that she wasn't ready for sex, but the guy shoved in her head that they were meant to be and that things would be fine.

And now, she had to deal with this.

But Donny made sure that Moe knew that she wasn't on her own. He was there for her. He was there for her in every choice she made.

He said that it was her idea to go to the clinic to deal with things. She thought that it would prevent things from getting worse, even though the guilt was eating her alive. He could see it all over her face. When the day had come and she made the choice to go in for her appointment, she practically cried before even entering the building. It didn't help that people were outside the clinic, calling her all sorts of names, making her feel sick to her stomach. It took everything in Donny's power to not slug anyone.

Donny and Moe had done everything in secret. It was just the two of them, after school that day. If their parents had known, or ever found out, they would've been slaughtered without a second thought. But Donny was with Moe the entire time. Even on the ride home, he'd hold her hand, think of all the right things to say, but he would end up saying nothing at all.

A few days go by and he noticed that Moe stopped taking her medication. He wanted to talk to her about it, ask if there was anything he could do to help her get back on track, but she was just silent. One evening after school, he came home and saw her lounging in the living room, looking at the television, but the television wasn't even on. He admitted that it frightened him a bit, seeing her stare at the black screen with such a deadpan face and droopy eyes. She hardly acknowledged his presence when he walked into the room, but there was nothing he could say to get her attention. It was as if her mind was in another dimension, and her body had been left behind.

Moe has been like that a few times, where Donny will come home or go into her room to check up on her, and she's just staring out in silence. He'd try to reason with his parents, hoping they'd take some kind of action in order to get Moe to take care of herself, but his mom would insist that there was nothing for them to do. Sometimes, their dad would go along with whatever their mother would say. Then there were times when their dad would actually speak-up and suggest something different. But neither one of their parents knew what to do when it came to Moe.

Donny said that not too long ago, there was a huge, terrible argument between Moe and their parents—mainly their mother. Donny doesn't remember much about how the argument started, or how things blew up so quickly. All he remembers is hearing Moe accuse them of favoring Donny over her, and she blamed their parents for everything that was wrong with her. Donny wanted to step in and tell Moe that things were going to be alright, but she'd probably swing at him since she sometimes gets violent when she's super-heated.

Fortunately, things started to dial down between all of them once Moe started taking her meds again. Occasionally. But then she'd attend her counseling sessions with Counselor Rashad, and Donny would attend his with Counselor Malik. The only reason Donny even signed up for counseling was because of Moe. Nothing against her, but he didn't want her to feel like she was the only one obligated to go. He wanted to show that he was there for her and that he wasn't better than her. He believed that he was far from being the better child.

"I wasn't the best brother, but I tried to be a good one." He twitched his nose, sniffing as a snowflake dropped on the ridge of his nose. He let out a sigh, closing his eyes. "I just wanted the best for her, you know?" His lashes fluttered open.

For a second, I definitely thought he was going to cry. His voice kept breaking, and he could hardly look at me when he spoke. I felt a sudden tightness in my chest that made it almost impossible for me to breathe properly. I took a deep breath.

Donny was a good brother. A damn good brother.

It's corny to say that no one is perfect, but who would want to be perfect anyway? You can be perfect and still suck at the same time. If you're perfect, there's no room for improvement, and you just do the same thing over-and-over again. People already know what to expect from you and it's hardly impressive.

I'd rather be considered *good* than *perfect*.

I think anyone would, to be honest.

So, I turned Donny's head so he was facing me. His eyes were a bit glossy, and he kept blinking to get rid of the tears that were forming in his eyes. It felt like a dagger piercing through my heart, seeing him this way. I rested my hand on his arm and looked him in the eyes as a faint grin took over my face.

"If 'goodest' was an actual word, and I looked it up on my search engine, I know that your face would pop-up instantly." I could hear my voice quivering as I spoke, so I cleared my throat, hoping that would help my words come out more clear. I was still looking Donny in the eyes as I said, "No doubt about it."

He snorted, smirking. "You sure have a way with words."

I shrugged. "I'm a writer, aren't I?"

He nodded. "Fair enough. At least you now know it." He suddenly jumped up off the ground, dusting off the back of his pants. "Maybe that'll be something you write about, you know?"

Donny then offered me his hand for me to take, and he helped pull me up off the ground. We locked eyes once I was standing with him. I curved my lips.

"Write about what? My '*way with words*'?" I snickered.

He rolled his eyes, crossing his arms over his chest.

"*That,*" he said, cocking his head to the side, looking away from me. "And also the fact that it took *me* having to drill into your head that you're actually good at what you do." His eyes shifted to me with one side of his mouth curving upwards.

He always had to be so blunt and cheeky.

I rolled my eyes. "You're truly something else."

He replied, "Yeah, well, I'm your something else, so take it or leave it, kid." He winked, clicking his tongue.

He walked past me and I could hear his soft chuckle as he headed back into the woods. At first I thought he was just trying to mess with me, acting all funny. But then I started to realize that he was probably right—saying that I was a good writer.

Even Mr. Rover thinks so too.

I never like to boast about my work, and I always think that I am okay. But I never actually thought I was *good*. Donny was the one who always brought up my writings, telling me that I was going places and was going to make a big name for myself as a writer. He always said those things as if they were true and destined. Maybe they were true. Maybe those things would happen for me.

Of course it'll take time, and I'll bring my family along with me wherever I go. But I couldn't take what he had said for granted, it'd be disrespectful. Disgraceful, actually.

By the time I got home, the street lights weren't even on and my mom wasn't home yet. Thank God. I thanked Donny for the ride, and then I unbuckled from the car seat. Donny dramatically tipped the non-existing hat on his head, saying it was his pleasure. I twisted my lips to hide the smirk on my face.

Donny threw back his head, laughing.

"That's why you're my favorite person, you know that?" His eyes remained on me as he sat back into his seat. "You're not afraid to let your hair down a little, even when you try not to, you still do.

It's kinda funny."

I took in the fact that he said I was his favorite person. He probably meant that I was "*one of his favorite people*", but the thought of being considered one of his favorites, period—it meant something. I thought about what Christopher had told me the other day, about Donny loving me. Not romantically, of course, but it did make me feel jittery when Christopher brought it up.

The truth is, I love Donny just as much.

It had nothing to do with the moment, or the fact that he was going to graduate soon and go to college overseas. None of that mattered. I mean, it mattered, but that's not why I loved him.

He was just Donald Gonzalez—the boy who asked to borrow one of my pens on the first day of school, and ended up becoming someone I actually wanted to know. Someone I desired as a friend.

Everything about him was epic. The good parts, the scary parts. Everything that made him...*him*.

So I told him, "You are the best, worst, most unpredictable person I know, Donald Gonzalez."

His eyebrows furrowed. "'*Worst*?'"

"Well, you're definitely no walk in the park, and you make my blood pressure go up unlike anyone else I know, so."

He snorted. "I guess I matter that much to you then, huh?"

I pressed my lips together and looked away from him when he flashed that cheeky, dimpled smile of his. That damn smile. It always gets me. But I never minded his smile. Honestly, I don't think I ever minded anything about him.

(Maybe some things, but not a lot.)

When I got out of the car, Donny leaned over to get a good look at me while buckled in his seat. He called out to me as I was heading up to my house.

"Hey, kid!"

I stopped in my tracks and looked back at him.

I heard him again. "I'll see you fresh on Monday. We got that test for Enrique still, right?"

A nervous chuckle. "Yeah, unfortunately."

Donny shook his head. "Don't worry, you got this."

"Says you! You ace every damn test you get." I took a couple steps closer to him as he groaned.

"Look, I'd bet my car on you with this one." He held his gaze on me as I made my way down to him. "Trust me, and you know my Golden Rule when it comes to my car."

(No food, no drinks—also, you don't mess around with his car.)

I nodded, telling him, "Yeah, I know."

With that, he winked, clicking his tongue. I watched him pull off, blasting the radio as his black vintage Cadillac car glided down the wide street. He was eventually out of sight, and everything became quiet.

I was about to head into my house when I spotted Benton, sitting outside his house. He was sitting on the porch steps of his house with his head downward. I thought something was probably up with him, so I went over to see how he was doing. I could see him swaying a little, and I soon noticed that his eyes were closed. As I got closer to him, I could hear him humming. I then noticed that his earbuds were looped in his ears.

When I tapped Benton's shoulder, he jumped and almost slipped right off the step. I had to cover my mouth to hide the smile on my face. Benton's face was hot pink as he took his right earbud out of his ear. His gaze was locked on me as he cleared his throat.

"H-H-H, how long have you been there?" he asked, pushing the front of his hair back.

"Only about a minute," I told him.

"Oh," he said, softly, while nodding his head.

He scooted over so I could sit next to him on the step.

"What'cha listening to?" I asked him.

He told me it was *November Sky* by Runaway Capsules.

It was one of their most successful singles, and I've listened to it a couple times. It's a great song—one of my favorites.

Anyway, Benton and I were sitting outside on his porch step, taking in the stillness of everything. He offered me his right earbud so I could listen to *November Sky* with him.

For a moment, everything seemed like a dream I once had. In my dream, I was admiring the beauty around me—a colorful sky, blissful silence, and it was just me, listening to one of my favorite songs while taking everything in. It sort of felt like déjà vu, but it could've just been a coincidence.

The moment sure felt right, though.

What's funny is that I didn't picture myself sitting there with Benton. I didn't picture myself with anyone, to be frank. It's a little strange but sweet irony at the same time.

Maybe that's something I could consider writing about for my essay—the one for Mr. Rover's class. Something about how irony can be bittersweet. To be honest, I don't know how I'm going to write this essay, or what I'll write about, but I know it'll get done. It's not like the idea will come to me overnight. I wish it were that simple. But it can't be that simple.

(It might defeat the purpose of the assignment, I guess.)

All I know is that today was a day of great reassurance. I still think a bunch of *what if's* and *how 'bouts*, but I think that's okay. I know often overthink things, but I truly believe that things will be just fine.

Anyway, it's getting late. Normally, I'd be up past midnight, working myself to death over my assignments, but I think some rest is well-earned. Take care of yourself. Talk to you soon.

Peace.

Your Friend,

Meagan Wright

A ~~Few~~ ^good amount of^ Words From the Author

I honestly don't know where to begin.

Well, I'd first like to begin by thanking God for blessing me with the idea of *We, pEOPLE*. This book has been a special part of my life for quite a long time. Since my junior year of high school, actually. Similar to Meagan, God has placed certain people in my life who have actually inspired me to write *We, pEOPLE*—a story about learning how to embrace certain changes in our lives. From saying goodbye to our old friends, then meeting people who you never expected to meet— life is never predictable. If it were, then we wouldn't really know what to do with ourselves. Even though I've probably written and re-written this book about a million different times, God always told me that something good would come out of it, and I believed Him all the way through.

I'd also like to thank my family for their support during this journey. My grandmother took the time to sit down with me and look things over before I decided to put this story out for you to read. My parents also looked out for me while I was on this wild ride. There were many times when my mom would come in my room and catch me still writing, and she'd tell me to get some sleep since it would be almost 2 AM. My dad would come in my room to check on me, and make sure I was alright. Even my little brother would sometimes barge into my room to see what I was doing. Sometimes, he would lean over my shoulder to read what I was writing.

Lastly, I'd like to thank all the wildcards out there. The ones who aren't afraid to show off to the nay-sayers, proving them wrong, while looking them dead in the eyes. The ones who are courageous enough to have an idea and run with it. The ones who wake up every morning and live their lives like an epic tale. It's truly wonderful to have so much ambition since we never know when it's going to be our last time to live. So having that courage, that drive—it means everything. It's in all of us. You just have to take a deep breath, and tell yourself: *You got this, kid.*

So I promise you, I truly am grateful for your support, and you are absolutely one of my favorite people. God bless.

AMARIS I. MANNING...

...was born and raised in Philadelphia, Pennsylvania, and has been living with a cardiac condition called Prolong QT Syndrome since she was born. She spends most of her days listening to music and writing stories while taking on the craziness of the world. She's an absolute anime and movie junkie, and she enjoys reading manga. She tries to do all she can to keep herself busy, otherwise she'll fall victim to taking a nap.

Photography by Charlotte Petitdemange

Made in the USA
Middletown, DE
24 December 2020